"Hold It Right There. Police!"

The woman spun away from the window, eyes wide with shock.

Marc's premonition of danger vanished like summer heat washed away by cool rain. The woman was unarmed, alone and heart-stoppingly vulnerable. There was a feeling in his gut as elemental as fear. *He wanted her.*

She reached her hand toward a pocket.

"Don't move!" He went up behind her and skimmed a practiced hand along her side to check for weapons. Through her thin cotton dress, he felt her quiver in response to his touch. The search should have been a standard, impersonal procedure, but he was aware, from his fingers through the rest of his body, that it wasn't.

This woman could play havoc with the control of a saint. And Marc Lasaralle was no saint.

Dear Reader:

Welcome to the world of Silhouette Desire. Join me as we travel to a land of incredible passion and tantalizing romance—a place where dreams can, and do, come true.

When I read a Silhouette Desire, I sometimes feel as if I'm going on a little vacation. I can relax, put my feet up, and become transported to a new world . . . a world that has, naturally, a perfect hero just waiting to whisk me away! These are stories to remember, containing moments to treasure.

Silhouette Desire novels are romantic love stories—sensuous yet emotional. As a reader, you not only see the hero and heroine fall in love, you also feel what they're feeling.

In upcoming months look for books by some of your favorite Silhouette Desire authors: Joan Hohl, Ann Major, Elizabeth Lowell and Linda Lael Miller.

So enjoy!

Lucia Macro
Senior Editor

FRANCES WEST

WHITE HEAT

SILHOUETTE *Desire*

Published by Silhouette Books New York

America's Publisher of Contemporary Romance

SILHOUETTE BOOKS
300 East 42nd St., New York, N.Y. 10017

ISBN: 0-373-05604-4

First Silhouette Books printing November 1990

All the characters in this book are fictitious. Any
resemblance to actual persons, living or dead, is
purely coincidental.

Books by Frances West

Silhouette Desire

Honky Tonk Angel #496
White Heat #604

FRANCES WEST

has been making up stories for as long as she can re-member. When she's not thinking about what she's just read, what she's writing or what she might like to write, she's traveling, studying ballet or playing her mandolin. Frances and her family live in Massachusetts.

One

Heat waves shimmered up from the worn pavement of the deserted parking lot, but in the sultry July afternoon, Brooke Shelburne shivered with a chill that couldn't be warmed by the sun. She pushed a strand of long, dark hair away from her face and glanced furtively over her shoulder. There was no one in sight.

The small magazine and tobacco store served by the parking lot was locked and empty, a Closed sign propped in the window. Brooke scanned the brick wall of the building. *What she was looking for had to be here somewhere.*

There was a single window, and Brooke moved stealthily toward it. The frame was wood, the paint peeling along the ledge. She ran her fingers over it, probing for loose mortar. Nothing moved under her investigating touch.

With a hurried glance over her shoulder, she crouched and searched the cracked asphalt for some crack or crevice large enough to hide what she was looking for: the small, spiral-bound notebook that seemed to have disappeared off the face of the earth.

Her father's patrol log. She had tried to put it out of her mind, along with all the nagging questions she'd tried—forced herself—to suppress. It hadn't worked. The questions had to be asked. And answered.

Brooke squeezed her eyes shut and took a shallow breath.

Bill Shelburne had been a good cop. In all the years he had been alive, she'd never had cause to doubt that. And she wouldn't start doubting now. She only needed some answers, some logical reasons....

Frustrated, she stood and leaned her hands against the window ledge. It had to be near here. Under the window was where her father had been when his partner had found him, slumped against the bricks.

Brooke clutched the edge of the ledge as the sense of loss overwhelmed her, and she felt sudden tears well in her eyes. She blinked them back. This wasn't the time for tears. And she wasn't that kind of woman, she thought fiercely.

Focusing on the dusty glass of the window, she noted the frame was locked in place with mortar and the window reinforced with steel webbing. It shouldn't have cost the life of her father to stop that break-in.

On impulse, she slammed the heel of her hand against the frame. One of the bricks moved. Brooke's heart started to pound. With excitement, she inched the loose brick away, leaving an empty space just large enough, she realized, to hold a logbook.

Brooke worked her fingers into the gap as far as she could, then, abandoning caution, pulled with all her strength on the next brick, determined to find the logbook she knew was there.

Detective Sergeant Marc Lasaralle pulled up at the intersection, scanned the main thoroughfare of Hartford's fifth precinct, and watched the driver of the station wagon next to them run the light.

"Geez, would you look at that?" Charlie Wilson, Marc's partner, pointed a thick index finger at the offending vehicle and shook his head in disbelief.

Halfway through the intersection, the young mother behind the wheel realized her mistake and slammed on the brakes. Her toddler's ice-cream cone wobbled precariously, and the family dog, draped halfway over the front seat, made a lunge for it. The distracted mother snatched the dog's collar with one hand and slowly backed up, peering nervously over her shoulder. The dog, Marc noticed, got in a couple of licks.

He grinned at his partner. "I think we ought to forget it, Charlie. I have a hunch it was just an ice cream problem."

"Okay by me. You're the one that gets all the magic hunches. Besides, it's too hot to be a cop today."

The radio squawked. Out of the police band unit, the static-wrapped voice of the dispatcher rasped the barely decipherable message: "Ten-fifty-nine, Lum's News and Tobacco, Park Street and River. Area units, please respond."

Marc exchanged a look with his partner.

Charlie's mouth quirked in disgust. "Ninety-five degrees outside and some s.o.b. is breaking into something," he said. "You got any hunches on that one, Marc?"

Marc grinned. "Yeah. I got a hunch no one else is going to take the call." He picked up the microphone. "Unit fifteen," he said into it. "We're on that ten-fifty-nine."

Charlie sighed, then muttered, "Let's go get 'em," and reached for the detachable police beacon to clamp it on the roof. Marc stomped on the gas pedal and made a hard left onto River Street.

A quick, sharp, familiar tingle of premonition snaked down his spine. It wasn't, he knew with sudden, sharp certainty, too hot to be a cop.

Lum's News & Tobacco, at the corner, looked deserted as Marc double-parked, shouldered open the car door, and got out.

"I don't hear any alarm," Charlie said, glancing at him.

"The building must be wired to headquarters. No on-site siren." He slammed the door. "Come on. Let's check it out."

Marc sprinted toward the corner, his partner following him. He halted abruptly before he reached the edge of the building. Charlie's heavy steps slowed, then stopped as he caught up to Marc. He gave his partner a wary glance.

There was someone there. Marc could feel it in his adrenaline-driven pulse and the trickle of sweat at the back of his neck.

"You cover the back," he flung over his shoulder to Charlie. "I'll check the side."

The empty parking lot, the most likely point of forced entry, was at the corner. Marc paused for the span of a heartbeat, then reached for the 9 mm automatic in his shoulder holster. He took a breath, then rounded the corner in police combat stance, his gun raised at arm's length in front of him.

"Hold it right there! Police!"

The girl spun away from the window with a gasp, one slim hand held to her throat, her eyes widening in shock.

Marc stared back at her, immobile, unable to speak, as shocked as she was. His premonition of danger vanished like summer heat washed by cool, drenching rain. The young woman was unarmed, alone, and, in the sights of his gun, immensely, heart-stoppingly vulnerable.

A cloud of dark hair spilled over her shoulders and framed her pale, oval face. Her slim body in the loose sundress was half turned toward him and rigid with stunned fear. She had wide gray eyes—the color of evening mist. Of water over gray stones. The color of rain.

There was another feeling in his gut, as elemental as his vanished fear but infinitely more complex, and infinitely less subject to rational explanation. *He wanted her.* Illogically, unreasonably, and against all the tough, streetwise tenets of police training, he wanted her.

She made a slight gesture of her hand toward her pocket.

He knew, in the span of time it took to form the thought, that she wasn't reaching for a gun, but the thought itself was enough to galvanize him into conditioned response.

"Don't move!"

She jumped at the barked order, and a small note-book spilled out of her pocket and dropped to the pavement at her feet in a flutter of fanning pages. She reached for it.

"Leave it there!"

The girl froze again. "B-but I—"

"Turn around and put your hands up against that wall. Do it! Now!"

He could hear the brutal harshness in his own voice: an overreaction to her effect on him. But he'd been a cop too long to let a pretty face and a surge of male hormones make him careless. He moved in behind her and kicked the notebook away, then skimmed a quick, practiced hand along her side, checking for weapons. She made a sound of dismay but didn't move until he bent to pick up the notebook. Then she turned her head and half reached for it again.

"Keep your hands up!" he barked at her. She drew in a sharp breath and snapped her head around to face the wall.

Picking the notebook up, he realized it was a stan-dard, police-issue patrol log, for recording police procedures and times, to be turned in at the end of each shift. Frowning, he tucked it under his arm, then reached for her again to run his hand along her other side.

When he touched her, she shivered and drew in a sharp breath. Marc made himself ignore her reaction. He ran his hand over her body in the prescribed search pattern. Through the thin cotton of her dress, he could feel soft flesh stretched over taut, tensed muscles that quivered in involuntary reaction to the pressure of his fingers. Her body curved in to a waist narrower than he would have expected, then swelled into the lush, feminine curve of her hip.

The search should have been a standard, impersonal procedure. He was aware, from his fingers through all the rest of his body, that it wasn't. His own swift masculine response shook him.

He stepped back and pulled his hand away so swiftly her dress billowed out as it followed the motion. "Okay, lady. Why don't you tell me what you're doing here?"

Charlie's heavy footsteps rounded the corner, then stumbled, as he came to an abrupt halt. "Oh... geez..." he muttered. Charlie reholstered his gun and let out a long, disconcerted breath. "You all right, Miss Shelburne?"

Marc flicked a look toward his partner before turning his eyes back to his suspect. "You know this woman?" he asked, surprise in his voice.

"Yeah." Charlie sighed again. "Marc, this is Brooke Shelburne. Bill Shelburne's daughter."

In the street behind them, the sound of a passing vehicle ruffled the startled silence, as Marc absorbed the information.

Brooke let her hands fall to her sides and slowly turned around. Her glance wavered for a moment between the two men, then she met Charlie's eyes and nodded. "I—I'm all right."

"Marc," Charlie said, his voice strained, "this is the place Bill Shelburne was shot to death."

The premonition that had visited Marc Lasaralle five minutes earlier expanded suddenly and sharply into a vivid picture, as if he had been witness to the event: the armed burglar, the quick shout of confrontation, the double explosion of bullets that had ended, in one shocking moment, the lives of an armed thief and a good cop.

Marc's gaze moved back to the woman he still held at gunpoint. A cop's daughter. Slowly, he lowered his gun and let out a breath. "Brooke Shelburne," he said.

Her chin rose and the gray eyes met his gaze. Her wide mouth was held rigid, but something in the fullness of the lower lip gave a hint of sensuality that evoked an elemental male hunger to explore it. The loose cotton dress fell straight from her shoulders to slight gathers at the hips, but he knew the way her body curved beneath the concealing cloth.

It was knowledge that would have played havoc with the control of a saint. And Marc Lasaralle was no saint. He was a man, and Brooke Shelburne was the kind of woman who made him want to forget everything else.

That wish shocked him. To cover it, he barked out a harsh identification: "Detective Sergeant Marc Lasaralle."

Her face showed fleeting, startled recognition. "Marc Lasaralle? The . . . psychic?"

It had been unintentionally blurted out, and her reaction was masked almost immediately, but Marc had seen the response too often not to recognize it: the curiosity, the shock, the tiny chill of superstitious fear. He felt a sudden surge of irritation at the reaction. Especially in a woman that stirred his senses the way this one did.

"You didn't answer my question, *Ms. Shelburne*. What are you doing here?"

She stared back at him for a moment, her breath coming in quick, shallow rhythm, her eyes wide with shock. "What am *I* doing here?" she said finally. "I'm standing in a parking lot, doing...doing *nothing* illegal. I'm being held at gunpoint and searched." Her gaze moved to the logbook under his arm. "You've taken my belongings with no reason. I've done *nothing* to justify this kind of—"

He cut her off brusquely. "You set off the burglar alarm, lady. This system's wired to headquarters. We're answering a call for a ten-fifty-nine."

"The...burglar alarm..." She glanced around at the window, then let out a dismayed sound of comprehension. The gray eyes flicked, half involuntarily, back to the logbook before she met his gaze once more. Her mouth tightened. She was wondering, he knew, how much he could guess of the truth. He was the enemy in her eyes, and he was aware, again, in a way that could threaten his police objectivity, that he didn't like it.

Charlie took a nervous step toward her and threw Marc an unhappy glance. "Uh...look, Miss Shelburne, there's obviously been a mistake made here. My partner just didn't realize..."

Charlie trailed off as Marc, taking his time, pulled the logbook out from under his arm, glanced down at it, flipped it open and fanned through the pages. Brooke made a sound in her throat that could have been protest, but Marc ignored it. When he looked up, his gaze was direct and cool. "This is department property, Ms. Shelburne," he said evenly. "What are you doing with it?"

"It...was my father's. And I'd like it back."

"It should have been turned in three months ago. Why wasn't it?"

"Hey, Marc." Charlie made a conciliatory gesture with one hand. "This is Bill Shelburne's *daughter*," he said, with slight but readable emphasis.

Marc returned the glance. "And that gives her a free hand to break the law?"

"I wasn't breaking any laws!"

His gaze swung back to her. He lifted the notebook, clutching it firmly in his fingers. "Police property, Ms. Shelburne."

A flare of color rose in her cheeks. Her fingers curled into the folds of her skirt in a visible effort not to snatch the logbook out of his hands. "I can explain that."

"I don't want a lot of complicated explanations. Just stick to the facts."

"It's not *complicated*," she said. "I've...had the logbook since my father died. I had it with me. I was thinking about him. I must have moved the window when I leaned against it. I..." She hesitated and her gaze wavered. "I'd like to have the book to remember him by."

There was a slight, husky catch in her voice that stroked Marc's body like the touch of a forbidden lover. And he'd been a cop too long not to know the danger in that response.

"You can go, Ms. Shelburne, but I'll keep the logbook."

"But I—" She flashed a look at him that held enough panicked desperation to alert his police training, but the look was gone almost too quickly for him to get a reading on it. He saw a flicker of something...explosive...in the gray eyes. Then Brooke Shelburne stepped away from him, turned to nod silently toward Charlie, and strode out of the parking lot toward the street. Her steps quickened to a hurried trot after she rounded the corner out of their sight.

Marc stood unmoving, listening to her footsteps.

"What the hell was that all about?" Charlie muttered sourly.

Marc turned toward him, shoulders squared. "She was trespassing with no reasonable explanation, Charlie. She went for her pocket. I wanted to know if it was a gun."

"Yeah, well, the chief's gonna love this one." Charlie's mouth quirked. He rubbed a hand across the back of his neck, under the limp collar of his shirt, then glanced up at his partner. "Her father got a posthumous commendation three months ago for being shot in the line of duty. And the chief's going to want to know why you—"

"The chief will have to live with it."

Charlie's long, exhaled breath was his only comment.

Marc met his partner's gaze levelly, reading his expression, then abruptly let his shoulders relax. "What was I supposed to do? Stand there like a lovestruck tomcat while she shot half a dozen holes in me?"

"You could have given her back the logbook. That's what she wanted."

Marc glanced down at the small notebook, jiggled it in his hand, then looked up at his partner again. "No. I couldn't."

"Why not?" There was a sudden, tense silence in the still, hot air of the parking lot. Charlie's gaze narrowed, and Marc felt his partner's swift, familiar reaction: alertness tinged with apprehension. "You got a hunch about this?" Charlie asked finally, his voice strained. "Some sort of...premonition?"

"I don't know."

Charlie sighed through his teeth. "Oh, geez." He shook his head. "You do, don't you? You got some sort of feeling about Brooke Shelburne."

"Yeah." Marc's voice was ironic. "I got some sort of feeling about her, all right."

Charlie studied him for a few seconds but made no answer. There wasn't much of an answer to be made, Marc knew. The truth was that, guilty or innocent of whatever crime may have been committed, Brooke Shelburne had knocked him so far off balance that he'd wobbled on the edge, half hoping for a fall. Nothing—no experience, no premonition—had prepared him for the intensity of his response to her when she'd turned toward him in front of the window. Dark hair like a cloud, gray eyes as changeable as water, the sensuous curves of a woman's body under the loose dress.

Just the thought of her alerted every male instinct he possessed. If he had any sense, he'd shut off the picture in his mind cold, cut off the feeling before it started, forget he'd ever met Brooke Shelburne.

He let out a breath, then looked toward the corner where Brooke had disappeared. *Forget her,* his inner voice warned.

He glanced back at Charlie, then rubbed a hand across the back of his neck. "I'm going to make sure she's all right," he said shortly.

Charlie's knowing sigh followed him as he strode away.

Two

Brooke got as far as her car, parked at the curb half a block from Lum's News & Tobacco, before she started to shake.

When she tried to insert her car key into the lock, her hands were trembling so much that she dropped the key ring. Frantic, she bent to pick them up, and the keys rattled in her fingers. She just wanted to get away from this place, to pretend she'd never met Detective Sergeant Marc Lasaralle, never been ordered at gunpoint to *turn around, put your hands up against that wall, don't move,* while she was frisked for weapons, the touch of his lean, strong fingers, callous, practiced, impersonal...

No. Not quite impersonal.

She dropped the keys again. She snatched them, straightened slowly, then propped her elbows on the hot roof of the car and covered her face with her hands, making herself take a deep breath. And another.

It would be all right. When Lasaralle had flipped through the logbook, he hadn't noticed anything wrong with it. Maybe there wasn't anything to notice. Maybe she should have left it where it was, never come here, never tried to find it.

Brooke whispered a curse into her fingers. Lasaralle hadn't quite believed her stammered explanation of what she was doing in a deserted parking lot with a police patrol logbook in her pocket, leaning against a window that just happened, by her bad luck, to be wired to an alarm. He'd made her feel like a criminal, damn him!

Stubborn, defiant Shelburne pride made Brooke lift her face and look around her at the crowded, prezoning business district of Hartford's fifth precinct. Her father's old beat.

Her gaze swept down the block of small stores toward Lum's News & Tobacco. The first time she'd seen it, she'd been ten years old, and it had struck her as disappointingly tame and safe, not at all the dangerous, violent place she'd seen before only through her mother's eyes—and her mother's fears. But those fears, it seemed, had been justified. Three months ago her father had been shot to death there, in a swift, senseless act of violence that had left her mother a helpless, dependent widow, and had left Brooke the burning compulsion never to become that kind of woman....

And five minutes ago, Marc Lasaralle had stood in front of her on that pavement and riffled through her father's logbook. There was an unwritten rule that the daughters of ex-policemen were treated with special courtesy, but apparently Marc Lasaralle hadn't heard of it. Or didn't care what the rules were.

The sharp edges of her keys dug into her palm. *No complicated explanations,* he said. *Just the facts.*

Well, that's what she had. The facts, no explanation. *Facts* were the white Lum's News & Tobacco envelope in her father's desk, smudged with brick dust and full of no-explanation fifty-dollar bills.

Facts were the logbook she'd found behind the window ledge just before Marc Lasaralle had stepped around that corner with his gun drawn. *Facts* were that Marc Lasaralle was top-notch cop with instincts so uncanny that they bordered on the paranormal.

Brooke squeezed her eyes shut and uttered a fervent prayer that Marc Lasaralle would never peruse that logbook and decipher whatever small secrets it had to tell. He would turn the logbook in to headquarters, and it would be filed away in the closed folder pertaining to her father's death, and maybe, somehow, she could get it back. She could invent a plausible story for some policeman who had known her father and owed his daughter a debt. And with any luck, she'd never again have to face the penetrating, arrogant gaze of Detetive Sergeant Marc Lasaralle and explain something unexplainable.

When she opened her eyes, he was standing on the sidewalk in front of her, his thumbs hooked into the belt loops of his tan chinos, the direct, dark gaze fixed on her across the roof of her car.

"Is everything all right?" he asked her.

The question was conventionally polite, but something about the man who asked it threatened to shatter whatever fragile control she'd mustered. She jerked her gaze away from him and clutched the keys more tightly in her hand. "Y-yes. I'm just fine." She got the key into the lock, but even over the noise of the street, the rattle of the key ring against the door was audible.

Marc Lasaralle had started around the back bumper before she got the door open. She watched him come toward her, unwillingly aware of the leashed power in the tall, lean body, while wild, improbable thoughts ran through her head. He was going to take her keys. Impound her car. Arrest her. Handcuff her and cart her off to jail.

"I'll drive you home," he said. He held out his hand for the keys.

Her fist tightened around them. "That's not necessary." There was a betraying catch in her voice she couldn't conceal. "I don't need any h-help."

Marc Lasaralle's dark, implacable gaze flicked down to her hands. She twisted them together to keep them from shaking, and willed herself not to take a step back from that overhelmingly masculine presence.

On the hot, sunbaked sidewalk behind Lasaralle, Charlie Wilson strode toward them. Brooke looked at the older man's heavily jowled, amiable face. It was easy to read the slight frown that creased his forehead: he'd known her father. He knew her. He believed in unwritten rules.

Charlie's eyes moved toward his partner. "You want me to call a cab?" Charlie asked.

Lasaralle frowned. "This time of day it will take half an hour for a cab to get here." He glanced back at Brooke in a swift appraisal that left no doubt of his opinion that she wasn't capable of the simple task of getting herself home.

"I don't n-need a cab," Brooke put in. "I'll drive myself. I'll be fine in just—"

Lasaralle's scowl cut off the sentence. His skeptical gaze moved over her face, then trailed down over the sundress to her hands, knotted in the folds of the skirt. Lasaralle's eyes fastened for a moment on her tensed fingers, then moved back up to her face in leisurely appraisal. Brooke knew the dress revealed little of her figure, but her figure was something Lasaralle knew intimately anyway. By touch.

Against her will, she felt a wash of heat paint her discomfiture across her cheeks for Marc Lasaralle to read in living color. And he didn't even have the decency to look away.

Blind, irrational fury shot through her. She was all the more outraged because she knew she wasn't entitled to feel that way. "I don't need any more of your help, *Sergeant*. You've done your job. Now why don't you just leave me alone? I can—"

"You can what? Get behind the wheel and head out on the road and check out your reflexes at fifty-five miles an hour?" His glance flicked over her again. "Sorry, Ms. Shelburne. That's not a good idea."

"I can assure you I'm not going to cause any accidents."

"No, you can't," he said.

"What?"

"You can't assure me that you're competent to drive."

Brooke made herself meet his eyes, buoyed by her anger.

He stared back at her, his mouth set. The force of that look was hard, unyielding and, in a way that made her pulse beat involuntarily faster, intensely, compellingly male. From the corner of her eye, she caught Charlie look from his partner to her and back again. The older man's frown was skeptical, half-resigned, and full of worldly assumptions.

All of which, Brooke told herself furiously, were way off base.

She made a supreme effort of will and bit back the reply that would have revealed her lack of control, then stated, "Look, you have no reason to concern yourself with how I get home. You can—"

"No. We're not leaving you here by yourself." The tone of his voice was determined enough to stop her in midsentence, and the words were arrogant enough to make her temper snap.

"You don't have the authority to keep me here!"

"Yes, we do, Ms. Shelburne," he said implacably. "We can keep you until that alarm's reset and the security on that building's back in place."

It took her a moment to realize what he meant: that the building had to be secured from *her*. Her jaw dropped and she stared at him, speechless.

Charlie muttered an indistinct curse.

Lasaralle ignored him. "Either we all wait here for a cab," he said evenly, "or I drive you home."

Brooke turned to Charlie. The older man glanced at his partner, obviously assessing the degree of deter-

mination in the aggressive posture, then looked back
to Brooke. He gave a slight shrug of apology and said
nothing.

On the sidewalk, a frankly curious ten-year-old
gawked at them while his more politely curious mother
hurried him along. Brooke tipped up her chin and
made herself match Lasaralle's stare. It appeared, incredible as it might seem, that she had no choice. She
could either insist on a cab and make them all stand on
the hot sidewalk while she endured a half hour of Detective Sergeant Marc Lasaralle's humiliating, unen-
durable surveillance, or she could salvage what was
left of her dignity and let him drive her home.

With no comment, she held out the keys.

The dark eyebrows rose in slight surprise as he took
them.

"All right, then, look . . ." Charlie said. "You take
her home in the squad car, and I'll follow you in hers."

Marc nodded. "What's your address, Ms. Shelburne?"

Brooke fought with the temptation to refuse to answer. She turned her head sharply away from him and
glanced down the street toward the unmarked police
car, with its blue flashing light still on the roof, parked
fifty feet from them. "Two seventy-eight Oakville
Street," she said brusquely, then turned her back on
the two policemen and strode toward the car. She
pulled open the passenger door to the front seat and
got in. She didn't want Lasaralle opening any doors
for her, then slamming them shut as if she were a
criminal being put in the back of the patrol car.

She leaned back in the seat, let out a long breath, then reached behind her to lift her hair off the back of her neck—and noticed what was on the seat.

The logbook was lying where it must have been tossed through the open window, next to her.

Brooke stared at it, her breath caught in her throat, her heart tripping in double time. Lasaralle was still involved in a discussion with Charlie, not looking toward her. Without a conscious decision, Brooke snatched up the notebook and flipped it open.

She scanned the pages hurriedly. There were the usual entries: police calls answered, suspicions investigated, normal activity on a police beat. There had to be something here!

She shot a frantic glance toward Lasaralle. He and Charlie still had their backs to her.

Her fingers awkward with haste, Brooke fanned through the logbook. The last page was dated April 11—the night of her father's death.

There was nothing unusual in the entry. The entire shift was neatly filled out with ordinary, unremarkable events. Frustrated, Brooke flipped back through the entries.

The entire shift. Brooke went still, and her heart rose into her throat. Her father had died an hour into his shift, but the log for that night had been filled out as if he had put in the entire eight hours. She flipped back to the last entry, wrinkling pages in her hurry. There was no mention, anywhere, of a burglary investigation at Lum's.

The entries had been falsified.

On an impulse, she tore out the page, her fingers fumbling with panic, and stuffed it into her pocket.

Her stomach was clenched into a knot when she shot a desperate glance toward Lasaralle, but he was still looking the other way. She snapped the logbook closed and set it back on the seat.

It was done. Marc Lasaralle hadn't seen her. In half a minute her heart slowed its frightened cadence, and Brooke felt a tiny thrill of satisfied triumph. She had done it. She had the clue she'd been looking for, though she didn't know yet what it meant. And nobody would be the wiser. Not even Super Detective Marc Lasaralle.

The elation lasted just for the time it took him to walk toward the car, open the door and get in.

Watching him, Brooke felt her relief evaporate like water sprinkled on hot pavement. He was looking at her as if he could see through her motives the way he could see through a windshield. As if she were transparent as a guilty child. *As if he could read her mind.*

The unbidden, superstitious thought made her heart start beating again in double time. Fighting panic, she made her voice work. "Take Farmington Avenue toward Elizabeth Park."

He returned her quick, self-consciously impersonal glance, nodded and pulled into the street.

Brooke kept her gaze fixed straight ahead and willed her attention away from Marc Lasaralle. It didn't work. The paper in her pocket seemed about to crinkle with every tiny move, and her own guilty conscience, shaped by twenty-four years of living on the right side of the law, was painfully conscious of the policeman sitting next to her. In the intimate space of the car, she sensed his presence in every cell of her body, and she felt a confusing, disconcerting mix of resentment, panic, and...some compelling force she couldn't quite define.

Because she didn't want to define it, she made herself glance at the man she'd known only by reputation before he'd charged around the corner with his gun drawn on her.

One arm was braced on the steering wheel. The ridges of muscle were delineated by the pale blue fabric of his polo shirt. His long legs didn't quite fit into the space afforded by the standard size car. Though his pants were loose, they did little to disguise the power of the masculine thighs. A pair of handcuffs hung from his belt, a stark reminder of what he was. She jerked her gaze away and studied his face.

Straight forehead, square jaw showing the shadow of a heavy beard, black hair, a little longer than it should have been, combed carelessly back as though he habitually raked his hand through it. She stared at the strong profile for half a minute before he turned to meet her glance.

One corner of his mouth quirked in an unexpected, ironic half-smile. "Do I pass muster?" he said.

With effort, Brooke made herself ignore the heat she felt in her face at the direct question. She didn't have to answer it, she told herself. Not here. She'd been faced down by Marc Lasaralle at gunpoint in a deserted parking lot, but she didn't have to accept his authority now, even if she was in a police car and he was driving it. She had the logbook page in her pocket, and Marc Lasaralle would never know it.

She unclasped her hands, which had been locked together in her lap, and propped an elbow on the window. "I suppose I should thank you for the ride home."

"But you're not going to, right?"

She stared back at him, her chin raised at a disdainful angle. "Thank you."

"You're welcome." There was a faint, surprising spark of amusement in the dark eyes. "Ms. Shelburne," he added.

She waited a few seconds, assessing the answer. "Will you get a lot of flak from your lieutenant because I'm Brooke Shelburne?"

"Yes, probably." He glanced at her again. "Does that make you feel any better?"

"It helps."

One corner of his mouth quirked up in the first sign of a smile she'd seen. It transformed his face, banishing the steely authority. But not the sense of hard, unalloyed masculinity.

She felt a shiver of response to something... dangerous... run down her spine and ignored it by sheer force of will. "You've taken a lot of flak before this, haven't you?"

This time he actually grinned, briefly, glancing upward for a second before he turned that ironic, not-quite-humorous glance toward her. There was a chip in the corner of one tooth that made a tiny gap between his front teeth and gave his grin an aura of innocence that was sharply surprising in the serious face. "The lieutenant and I have a working relationship."

"I'll bet you do."

One brow rose. "You doing research on me? Or is this just idle curiosity... Brooke?"

On her name, his voice dropped to a low-pitched murmur, rich with something she couldn't distinguish—intimacy, challenge, or both. Her own shiver of response was disquieting and unexplainable, but she didn't have enough control of the situation to let herself think about it.

"I don't have to do any research to know that much," she snapped. "I've done some PR work for the Hartford Police. You have a pretty wide reputation on the force."

He let out a huff of near-laughter. "Maybe I should be flattered. How long have you been working for the department?"

"For as long as I've been free-lancing. A little more than three months."

"Three months. Who have you been talking to?"

Brooke gazed back at him while his dark gaze flicked over her. "Department gossip has it that you don't go by the book," she said, her voice too quick, the tone too nervous. "That you have your own . . . individual interpretation of department policy, that you get a lot of . . . spontaneous flashes of intuition."

He gave her a skeptical glance, one eyebrow raised. "What are you trying to get at? That I'm a *psychic*?"

A muscle in her cheek tightened and she straightened. The word hung in the air between them, fraught with eerie connotations. She had a sudden, sharp sense of why she hadn't wanted to say it. Unnerved, she blurted out, "Is it true?"

Marc Lasaralle glanced in the rearview mirror, slowed for a yellow light, then pulled up as it changed to red. "Yes," he said finally.

"I see."

He glanced at her, frowning in assessment. "If you don't like the answer, *Brooke*, you shouldn't have asked."

"If you don't like my reaction, you shouldn't have answered," she snapped. "I don't imagine there are very many people who *would* like being told that they're in the company of someone who can read minds."

"I can't read minds."

Brooke was silent, staring at his profile.

He glanced toward her. "I'm not some sort of alien in human disguise." The words were casual, but there was a hint of anger underneath them. She had a fleeting realization of the very human hurts that must have caused that anger, but she cut off the thought with sharp finality. She couldn't afford sympathy. Sympathy for Marc Lasaralle, like honesty, was another luxury of innocence. It was too dangerous.

"You're not exactly 'normal', either," she said.

He didn't lose his temper. "Everyone has a certain amount of psychic ability. I have more than most. Not enough to qualify as a mind reader." The dark gaze touched her again, swiftly and surely, then swung away.

In spite of herself, Brooke slipped her hands into her pockets and dug her fists down deep into the material. The folded page was beneath the fingers of her right hand, and she had to suppress the impulse to crumple the paper into a tiny ball. "Whatever you call it, that's the way you solve cases?"

"I solve cases by hard work and persistence, like any other cop. Sometimes I get a lucky hunch. It still doesn't make the job easy."

Brooke pushed her hands farther into her pockets and stared at the windshield, telling herself she wasn't afraid of Marc Lasaralle's "psychic" hunches and trying to pretend she wasn't Marc Lasaralle's latest case. "If the job is so hard, why do you do it?" she asked.

"Because it's worth doing. Because I'm suited to it, no matter what you might be thinking to the contrary, Ms. Shelburne."

"Oh, I think you're suited to it," she said grimly. "I can't imagine you as anything but a cop."

"Is that a compliment?"

"No."

She caught the edge of his ironic grin and a glimpse of the chipped tooth, and was surprised by the unexpected urge to ask him what he was thinking of, before she snapped her head around to the window and stared at the road.

The sign for Elizabeth Park was ahead of them. Marc Lasaralle slowed and flicked on the blinker. It blipped rhythmically into the silence.

"You have a funny attitude for a cop's daughter," he commented.

"I have a funny *attitude* for a cop's daughter?" she flared at him. "All cops' wives and kids are supposed to have the same attitude, as if it's handed out like a police-issue uniform? And let me guess what it should be—unquestioning support and admiration, and just don't ever mention the violence and the danger."

Marc Lasaralle gave her a look that made her regret, immediately and intensely, the unguarded words. "You didn't want to be a cop's daughter?" he said almost softly. "That's why you kept your father's logbook to remember him by?"

She stared at him, eyes wide in the strained, tense silence of the patrol car. Lasaralle took the turn toward her street without asking for directions and without breaking the silence.

"My father was shot to death three months ago, Sergeant," she said finally. She'd meant to sound outraged, but there was a tremor in her voice that, for all she didn't want to reveal it, she couldn't control.

Marc Lasaralle gave her another long, level glance. "I know that," he said finally. "And I'm sorry."

The sensitivity in the rough voice was not what she expected. To her horror, she felt quick, unexpected tears well behind her eyes and a lump of emotion rise into her throat. She bit down hard on her lip and turned her face toward the passenger side window.

He took the turn onto Oakville. The familiar, shaded street, lined with white clapboard Victorian homes now converted to apartments flowed by the window, blurred by her misted vision.

"Don't get into trouble with this, Brooke," he said behind her.

The quietly spoken words shocked her into facing him again. "I haven't...done anything to get into trouble over!"

"You were apprehended on private property with no specific reason to be there, Brooke. You set off a burglar alarm. You had a police patrol logbook that's illegal to possess in your pocket. And right now, you're hiding something.''

She started. Involuntarily, her fist closed around the page in her pocket. "I told you what I—"

He cut her off. "Right. And I don't have any reason to disbelieve you. Yet.''

She stared back at him, unable to formulate any response, while her pulse raced along like a fugitive fleeing pursuit, and Marc scanned the street for her apartment.

The number of the house was on the door. He found it without her assistance, parked expertly in the small space left in front of the house, and shut off the car.

Brooke got out and slammed the door before he could say anything more. She was home, she told herself, safely off the road and out of his custody. And nothing on earth would make her spend any more time with him. She'd wait at the curb for Charlie, get her keys and forget about Marc Lasaralle and his uncanny guesses.

He got out of the car and stood beside her on the sidewalk. He was near enough so that she could smell the faint, clean scent of soap and hear the faint squeak of holster leather as he stretched his shoulders. His tanned arm, dusted with black hair, was inches from hers. The muscles looked as hard and tough-sinewed as carved wood. His hands, looped in the belt of his chinos, were strong, long-fingered, and very clean. And half an hour ago, he had traced the curves of her body with them as he searched her for weapons.

Brooke shut her eyes, swallowed hard and turned toward him. "Would you tell Detective Wilson to leave my keys with the landlady downstairs?'' she asked. ''I'm going in.''

''I'll walk you to the door.''

''No, thank you, Sergeant,'' she said through gritted teeth.

The dark eyes gazed back at her, with the intense, unblinking assessment that made his stare so unsettling. In spite of herself, her gaze faltered, and she closed her fist tighter around the logbook page. Marc Lasaralle, she knew, didn't miss that.

Furious with herself for that slip, she clamped her jaw shut and turned her back on him. She rang her landlady's bell and borrowed the extra key to let herself into her apartment, leaving Marc Lasaralle standing on the sidewalk waiting for his partner. But, superstitiously, she didn't take out the crumpled page to look at again until Charlie had come in the patrol car, and she'd watched them pull away from the curb and disappear at the end of her street.

Three

___

He was called by a vision, and it would lead him straight into the fire.

Marc Lasaralle knew, with some part of his consciousness, that he was dreaming, but the woman who stood before him in the shadowy space of his mind was not the stuff of any ordinary dream. The sense of her presence was so real he could hear the faint sound of her indrawn breath and the rustle of her dress as she spun around toward him, startled, one hand clutched at her throat.

The cloud of dark hair was back-lit by some flickering light whose source was hidden from him. The curves of her slim body, inside the loose sundress, were just vaguely defined by the light. She looked back at him through wide, rain-gray eyes—and he was mesmerized by that gaze.

Behind her, in the direction she had been facing, the direction of the flickering light, he knew there was danger. He could sense it, and he knew, too, that in some way she was calling it to her. Sooner or later it would engulf her. She would be drawn into it like a rush of air sucked into a furnace, and anyone who stood close to her would be sucked in with her.

But he couldn't look away from those eyes. He didn't want to. He reached toward her, took a step.

Her hand was cool and trembled in his, and the gray eyes met his gaze with an innocence that drew him as inexorably as his sensual response to her. His fingers closed around hers.

Without warning, flames shot up around them in raging, terrifying heat. He thought she cried out—his name, or a call for help. He tried to answer, but his voice stuck in his throat, his pulse pounded in his ears and the flames blinded him....

Marc sat up, thrust into wakefulness by his own adrenaline-driven heartbeats. He was naked to the waist, the sheet tangled around his hips, and he was drenched in sweat. *Brooke Shelburne.* The name was an echo in his mind, as vivid and disturbing as the dream. And the sense of her presence lingered with him, impossible to shake off, impossible to dismiss from his intense emotions. It had been a vision, no doubt, called by his own desires. And something in him didn't want to let it go.

The dark room was stifling. The curtains, just visible at the open window, were still, unruffled by any breath of wind.

Marc wiped the back of his hand across his forehead and shook off the emotions of the dream. The strange, unsettling sense of dual reality would pass. He'd had dreams like this before—vivid, real, somehow prescient. There was no point in racking his brain for meanings or portents. It would come clear to him, or it wouldn't, in its own time. But sleep would be impossible, he knew. He pushed back the tangled sheet and stood up, then paced to the window, leaned his palms on the sill and stared out into the hot night.

Somewhere out there was a reality that covered its acts in darkness. The drug dealers, vandals, thieves petty and not so petty. It was his business to find them.

Somewhere out there, too, was a woman who, for reasons as mysterious and ancient as the darkness, made him burn with the primitive, powerful, irrational desire to possess her.

He wasn't sure which was more dangerous.

Brooke drank half a glass of wine, ate the last potato chip in the bag, then sat in her darkened kitchen in the middle of the night and admitted to herself that Marc Lasaralle scared her.

She wiped the crumbs from her fingers, crumpled the empty potato-chip bag into a ball, and tossed it toward the wastepaper basket. It bounced off the rim. Brooke let out a sigh and buried her face in her hands.

The logbook page was on the table in front of her, creased from being in her pocket, most of it covered with her father's distinctive printing. Brooke stared at it, then raked her hands through her hair and raised her face toward the window, where the hot darkness pressed against the screen like damp black cotton. The air was so still and oppressive it seemed charged with the potential for violence. *Trouble weather,* her father had always called it. All cops hated it.

She felt a lump rise in her throat, and for what seemed like the thousandth time, her eyes misted with scalding tears. An ache of grief knotted in her chest. Bill Shelburne had been her father, counselor, teacher. She'd fought against his overprotective care, pitted her own stubborn nature against his equally stubborn views—but all her life she had assumed the simple, clear-cut values of a policeman's daughter: right and wrong. Black and white. She'd never questioned the fact that her father was on the right side of the law. The side that didn't allow uneasy compromises with the truth. Marc Lasaralle's side.

Brooke felt a shiver run down her spine, as palpable as the touch that had traced the outline of her body through the thin material of her sundress. She had stood there, this afternoon, her father's logbook on the pavement at her feet, her hands pressed against the brick wall, and felt a stirring of something that made her breath catch in her throat. Something...dangerous.

She couldn't afford to feel anything for Marc Lasaralle. She had a secret to keep.

Brooke squeezed her eyes shut, shivering again in the heat. She could picture her mother's shocked, anxious face, if Millie Shelburne ever learned where her daughter had been, what she had been doing, what she had been thinking....

Don't tell Mom. It was a litany she'd heard since childhood. *Don't tell Mom Pop's thinking about working the night shift. Don't tell your mother about*

that little bit of trouble on River Street. Don't tell
Mom that Pop's been assigned to the Fifth Precinct.

They'd all tried to protect her. To shield her—as if
they could—from her overwhelming, ever-present fear
that one day the husband she depended on for everything would go out to work and not come home...

Impulsively Brooke reached for the phone. She
dialed her younger brother's number from memory.
Billy was a nighthawk, and it was a Friday night. It
was likely he'd still be up. And she had to talk to
someone.

He picked up on the third ring. "Bill Shelburne,"
he said into the phone.

The unnaturally deep voice, saying her father's
name, trying so obviously to sound like her father,
stopped her cold for a moment before she managed to
ask, "Billy?"

"Sis?" The pitch went up half an octave.

"Yes. You're still up?"

"Yeah." He sighed. "Studying. I've got an exam in
criminal law tomorrow."

"On...Saturday?"

A chuckle came through the phone. "I'm in the
Police Academy, Sis. The only time they don't have
classes is on Sunday mornings, when you're supposed
to study on your way to church. I've got another
hundred pages to memorize before I get to go to bed.
They don't believe cops need sleep. So, how come
you're still up?"

Brooke's glance fell to the crumpled page in front
of her. Her hand gripped the receiver more tightly.
"I...couldn't sleep," she got out. "It's too hot. And

I was thinking how Pop always hated hot weather like this, and I—'' She broke off, biting her lip.

"Yeah," Billy said.

A sudden, sharp picture formed in Brooke's mind: her father, in the passenger seat of the car they'd owned when she was sixteen, leaning across the seat to tap his finger on the speedometer and chewing her out about exceeding the speed limit. *Thirty miles an hour,* he'd said. *That doesn't mean thirty-five!*

She stared at the crumpled piece of paper in front of her. *And it didn't mean a falsified log, either,* she protested silently. *Did it?*

"Billy, I—"

"Yeah, I know," Billy said, his voice rough with emotion. "I think about him all the time. I miss him, too, Sis. Sometimes I just can't understand how someone who was that good a man could have died that way. It just...isn't fair, you know?"

Brooke squeezed her eyes shut and pressed the plastic edge of the receiver against her forehead. She couldn't tell Billy, any more than she could tell her mother. To Billy, her questions and doubts would be unthinkable.

Brooke's shoulders slumped in defeat. Maybe she was the one who was wrong. Maybe she was betraying everyone—her father, her family...

"Brooke...Brooke...?"

She put the phone back to her ear. "Yes. I'm still here."

"You okay?"

"Billy, do you know anything about Marc Lasaralle?"

She hadn't known she was going to ask it. The surprised silence over the line was half hers. Billy let out an unexpected breath of awed admiration. "Yeah," he said. "He was a guest speaker in my criminal law class. He's one of the best. When he gets onto a case, he can't seem to miss." There was another pause, then Billy added. "They say he's—"

"—psychic," Brooke finished for him.

"Yeah." Her brother's tone held more than a hint of hero-worship. "He's a damn good cop. One of the best."

Brooke said nothing for a moment. Billy had stopped short of saying, *Just like Pop,* but she knew without asking that it was what he meant.

"Hey—" Billy started, a familiar note of kid-brother joshing in his voice. "You don't have a thing going with Marc Lasaralle, do you?"

"No! Of course not. I just met him. I've been doing a . . . press release. It's just business."

"Oh? Business?"

She cut off the teasing with a sharp, "Look, just forget I mentioned him, okay? Please."

Billy's uncertain, "Yeah, okay," told her clearly that her tone of voice had been just as sharp as she'd heard it to be. "Billy—" Brooke let out a sigh. "I stopped by to see Mom yesterday. She said you'd been there and changed a fuse. She said she wouldn't know what to do without you."

"Yeah. She didn't even know where the fuse box was. Pop always—"

"I know," Brooke said. There was a pause. "Well, good luck on your exam, okay?" she put in, trying for a smile.

"Yeah, I'll try. Thanks, Sis."

She hung up feeling worse than before she'd called and with another niggling burden of guilt to add to her store. She shouldn't have snapped at her brother, shouldn't have let his innocent, misguided question get to her. Angry at herself, she snatched up the page on the table and crumpled it in her fist.

So why had she?

She stared at her clenched fist in the half-darkness.

She'd let Billy get to her because she felt guilty. Because Billy, her mother, her father's old partner—all of them—could be devastated by the evidence she held in her hand and the suspicions she had in her mind. Because family loyalty meant she should have left it alone, never gone to that parking lot, never found the logbook, never been apprehended and searched—

Brooke cut off the remorse-laden voice in her own head, got up from the table and poured herself another glass of wine. Slowly she smoothed out the crinkled page, pressing it down against the kitchen counter, staring at it, trying to find the thread of self-knowledge in her own confused thoughts.

That's what her mother would have done. Left it alone, stifled the questions, accepted the soothing, well-meaning platitudes. But there was something in Brooke that rebelled against that dependence. She needed to know the truth, whatever the cost.

Impulsively she folded the logbook page and slipped it under the phone book on the kitchen table. No edges showed; it was hidden, but somehow that fact did nothing to calm her agitation. She took another nervous gulp of wine, stared at the phone, then shut her

eyes and silently faced an uneasy truth on her long list
of uneasy truths: Marc Lasaralle scared her.

He scared her because he was a good cop.

And she was on the wrong side of the law.

Brooke woke suddenly with the sharp, subcon-
scious knowledge that something had wakened her.
She stared into the darkness of her bedroom, listening.

For thirty seconds she heard only her own breathing, then the muffled, threatening thud she'd heard in
her sleep.

The back of her neck went rigid. Her straining sense
of hearing caught a soft scraping that could have been
a heavy foot on the living-room rug, then the almost
inaudible rattle of paper.

A panicked, primitive fear tightened her chest.
There was someone in her apartment.

Frantically she scanned the dark room. French
doors opened onto a rooftop terrace, lined with the
potted plants of her herb garden, but the edge of it was
a two-story drop to the walkway below. The only way
out of her bedroom was through the door that now
stood closed tightly.

Her heart started to pound. *Someone had closed her
bedroom door.* Her heart racing, she slid out of bed,
making herself move slowly enough so the mattress
wouldn't creak. She couldn't stay here, waiting in ter-
ror for that door to open.

But what could she do? The portable phone she
usually carried into the bedroom had been left in the
office.

Desperate, she looked around for something that would serve as a weapon. Books, lamp, bureau drawer? A furtive scrape from the living room made her snap her head around toward the door. She let out her breath.

Aerosol hair spray. The old, unused can on her bureau was scant defense, but it was the best she could find. She silently crossed to the bureau and picked it up. Clutching the can, her finger on the spray button, she moved toward the door.

In the living room, muffled footsteps crossed the rug. The floorboard in the middle of the room squeaked, and the steps paused. In the silence, Brooke made herself stay rigid, afraid even to move her hand the inch toward the doorknob.

The steps moved again, across the room toward her office. She thought she heard the office door scrape across the carpet.

Now. Go now.

Even with the internal command clamoring in her mind, Brooke waited precious seconds before she could make herself touch the knob, turn it, inch the door open.

The hallway was pitch-black. She stared intently toward the kitchen. She could see the room in her mind. It was just a dozen steps to the back door. She could get to it, unlatch the chain, and be down the back stairs before he heard her, she told herself.

Now.

She took a step into the hallway, looking over her shoulder toward the dark living room. She took another two steps. She could make it.

She made a furtive dash for the door—and her bare foot struck something that shouldn't have been in her path. Brooke went down hard in a deafening clatter of wooden chairs. The spray can flew out of her hand and hit the floor, and on the other side of the apartment, as if in answer, she heard the splintering of breaking porcelain and the heavy thud of footsteps.

She scrambled toward the back door and fumbled desperately with the chain. Across the dark living room, a tiny flashlight beam lit a path, then her front door was yanked open. Running footsteps pounded away down the front stairs to the street.

Brooke stood where she was, holding the doorknob, listening to the retreating footsteps, then the silence. Finally she let out a single, convulsive sob and sagged against the wall. She groped for the light switch, stumbled toward the phone and picked up the receiver.

Marc Lasaralle flipped the file folder closed on the scarred metal work table and stared at it for a moment, thinking.

Shelburne, William F., Sergeant.

Marc ran his hand through his hair and leaned back in the uncomfortable, straight-backed chair in the station's file room.

Thirty-one years on the force. Married for twenty-eight of them. A son in the police academy. And a posthumous commendation for losing his life in the line of duty.

He tapped his knuckles on the top of the folder. He'd learned damn little else. According to his file, Bill Shelburne had been a cop like most cops. Overworked, underpaid and with not enough vacation time. He'd played on the softball team and died without using one hundred and thirty-eight accumulated sick days. His son was a first-year student at the police academy. His partner, Pete Carter, had taken early retirement after Bill had been shot.

And his daughter had been caught setting off an alarm in a wired building, with his patrol log in her pocket.

Brooke Shelburne's image flashed in Marc's mind, and he felt his physical reaction to it in the heat that rose through his body. The dream that woke him had been so vivid he could have reached out and touched her—run his hand through her hair, down the soft, vulnerable curve of her neck, under the collar of the filmy, semitransparent dress. *That was what he'd needed to put himself back to sleep—an hour with Brooke Shelburne in, and out of, a transparent dress.*

And maybe that was all that had caused the dream. Maybe his own physical needs were the only reason he was sitting in the station in the middle of the night, staring at a file folder that had nothing to tell him, and drinking lousy coffee from a plastic cup.

The door behind him opened. Jack Mason, the nightshift desk cop, poked his head into the doorway. "Lasaralle?"

Marc glanced at him over his shoulder.

"You wanted to be kept informed about anything that had to do with that ten-fifty-nine this afternoon?"

Marc twisted in the chair, leaning it back on two legs, his arm over the metal back. "Yeah. I did."

"The Shelburne girl—the perp? She just called 911. Someone broke into her apartment."

The chair banged down onto the floor. Marc pushed himself up from the table, one hand on the file folder. "Who's on dispatch?"

"Duran," Mason said.

Marc crossed the room and brushed by the shorter cop, asking over his shoulder, "What do they know?"

Mason shrugged. "That's it." As Marc sprinted down the hall toward the desk, he added, "You can ask Duran."

Eleven minutes later Marc turned onto Oakville Street and flicked on his high beams, automatically scanning the street for signs of disturbance. It was as quiet as a church on Saturday night. The only lights on the street were in the house at the other end of it, where Brooke's apartment was located. That was lit up like a Christmas tree.

He glanced at the dashboard clock as he pulled into a parking space as close as he could get to her address. Three twenty-five. She'd called at 3:18, when, according to Duran's sketchy report, she'd discovered the break-in. Marc felt his hands tighten on the steering wheel and an irrelevant question form behind his clenched teeth. Where had she been until 3:18 in the morning? Out on the town? With a lover? Wearing some semitransparent nightgown...letting her dark hair fall like a cloud against some other man's chest?

He let out a wry huff of breath. *She'd been invading his dreams, that's where.* The reality of where she'd been was none of his business. His business was answering a police call for a breaking and entering report.

He got out of the car and started toward the house, walking briskly.

It was none of his business unless he made it so, the way he'd made this call his business. The way he'd reached out to her in his dream.

He felt a warning prickle along the back of his neck: the elusive, never-quite-familiar urgency of premonition. His steps quickened.

The downstairs lights were on. She must have wakened the landlady. Aware that he wasn't in uniform, Marc went around the house to the back stairs, which led to Brooke's private entrance. He jogged up the stairs, pressed the door buzzer and heard footsteps from the apartment.

The door opened and Brooke Shelburne stood framed in the doorway, one hand on the knob, her surprised gaze widening as she stared back at him. She made a sound that was not quite a gasp, then swallowed hard and found her voice.

"Sergeant Lasaralle."

"Ms. Shelburne." She was wearing a loose, pale green long-sleeved T-shirt, jeans and running shoes. She had no makeup. He wondered if it was how she'd looked when she was out. He caught a faint, aromatic herbal scent, but he didn't know if it was her perfume or something in the apartment. "Can I come in?" he said finally into the lengthening silence.

She was still staring at him, her eyes wide and wary. "I was expecting a patrol car," she said. Her voice was a husky, hesitant contralto that spoke to all his masculine responses at the same time that it betrayed her nervous hesitance. "How did you . . . happen to take the call?"

He met her gaze, aware of the rising heat in his body, wondering what she'd say if he told her, *I'm here because you walked into my dreams and set us both on fire.* "I was in the station," he said. "I told the desk I'd take it."

He saw her breath go out, beneath the curve of her breasts in the T-shirt. He could almost feel the faint relief: no psychic phenomena to account for here.

He let out his own breath and stepped into the room. She turned to watch him as he entered the kitchen, gave the undisturbed room a cursory check, then went through to the living room. He glanced around, frowning. The room looked as if it had been ransacked by a burglar with a neatness compulsion. Books were pulled off their shelves and stacked in piles, chair cushions had been methodically tipped on end, records and tapes sat on the floor in front of the stereo cabinet. The sweet, enticing scent of herbs was stronger here. Across the small hall he could see the open door to her bedroom—a lacy bedspread, green, leafy plants.

His gaze flicked back to Brooke. "Was anything taken?"

She shook her head. "Not much. Some money from my wallet . . . fifteen dollars . . ."

He took a couple of steps toward a doorway that opened into an office. It had been ransacked in the same way as the living room. Brooke hesitated, then followed him into the living room.

"You didn't have your wallet with you?" he asked.

He could feel her frown. "My purse was on the coffee table, I think. When I came out, I found it on the floor."

He turned toward her, his mind clicking into high alert, and he felt tension gather along his neck and shoulders. "When you came out of *where*?"

She gestured with her hand. "The bedroom."

He felt a muscle in his jaw clench. She'd been in her bedroom while some son-of-a-bitch trashed her apartment? A surge of irrationally charged anger tightened the muscles of his chest and arms. "Someone broke in here while you were asleep?" Even in his own ears, his voice sounded like granite.

She blinked at him, and her face paled in the brightly lit room. She wrapped her arms around herself protectively. "Y-yes."

"Were you alone?"

The question came out of his mouth before he'd realized he was about to ask it. There was a flicker of faintly outraged surprise in her face.

"Yes."

All his instincts told him to cross the room toward her, pull her into his arms and comfort her the way he had done in the dream. The way he'd wanted to hold her and comfort her the first time he'd seen her. The way he wanted to hold her forever.

He wrenched his gaze away from her, turned abruptly and strode back through the kitchen toward the phone.

There was a tense silence in the apartment while Marc Lasaralle dialed the number and waited for an answer. Brooke stood staring at his back. His blue chambray shirt was stretched taut across his shoulders. The sleeves, rolled up to the elbow, revealed the ridge of muscle in his forearm, as he held the receiver to his ear. Even beneath the material of his shirt, she could see the line of his back was rigid with tension. She loosened her own shoulders with conscious effort and shut her eyes, trying to make sense of her reaction to Marc Lasaralle.

Her call to the police had been a first response. Second nature. Something she'd absorbed along with nursery rhymes. When you were in trouble, you called the police.

But she hadn't expected the call to be answered by the man who had caught her setting off a burglar alarm and made her feel like a criminal. *Don't get into trouble,* he'd told her. *You're hiding something,* he'd said....

She opened her eyes and focused on Lasaralle, who stood in front of the kitchen table, the phone to his ear. Under the phone book before him was the page from her father's logbook. And Marc Lasaralle was—

In a sudden panic she made herself look away and forced her thoughts onto something else. The word *psychic* seemed to echo as if she'd said it aloud.

"Yes," he said abruptly into the phone. "This is Lasaralle. You've got a mistake on the seven-fifty-eight reported earlier on Oakville Street. She was here when he broke in. I want it reclassified as trespassing with threat, and I want someone here to dust this place for prints. Who's on?"

Brooke glanced back toward him, startled.

"All right," he said. "Get him over here." He let out a breath, raised his eyes to the ceiling for a moment and shifted his weight. "I'll think of one. Tell him I said so. I'll wait."

He glanced over his shoulder toward Brooke. His gaze struck her like a tiny jolt of electricity.

"Okay," he said suddenly into the phone. "Thanks." He started to swing back toward the table, then stopped. "Yeah? What is it?" There was a silence, then he went rigid. She saw the telltale muscle in his jaw clench, and he turned his back to her. "Yeah," he said again. The word was short and harsh. "Thanks."

He put the phone down carefully, staring at it for a moment before he turned around. When he faced her, his expression was carefully neutral, his voice even. "There'll be someone here within a couple of hours to dust for prints."

Brooke nodded, apprehensive, waiting for him to explain the sudden, grim reaction to whatever he'd been told.

The black eyes flicked over her face. "How did they get in?" he asked brusquely.

"I . . . don't know."

"Was the lock forced? Is there a window broken?"

"I don't think so." She looked toward the front door, then the kitchen. It caught for a moment on the phone book, and she shifted her eyes, guilty. "I don't know how they got in." His gaze was on her face. It was unnerving. *He knew she had something to hide.* Did he think she was lying now? "I don't *know*," she blurted out. "Maybe they picked the lock. Or maybe it's possible I . . . left the door open."

"You go to sleep at night without locking your door?" he said.

A swift, instinctive flicker of defiance gave her the starch to resist him. "It's my door. If I forget to lock it at night, that doesn't make me a criminal!"

She saw a muscle work in his face. He moved toward her and the iron grip of his hands closed around her shoulders. "Do you have any idea what kind of trouble you could have been in? There are crooks out there who make the cops look like Mary Poppins. Your landlady could have been the one to call the police, just before she had you taken away to the morgue."

The words were as deliberately shocking as his grip. Brooke's teeth clicked together in an involuntary reaction that left her speechless.

He didn't stop. "So you're going to start locking your door, Brooke," he ordered. "And you're not going to open it to anyone without asking for ID. You're going to make sure the landlady is home, and when she isn't, you're going to call one of the neighbors and have them keep an eye on this place. You're going to start cooperating with the law, because that's your best shot at staying healthy."

His grip was so tight, she was raised on tiptoe, her eyes almost level with Marc Lasaralle's black gaze, her face inches from his. She could feel her heart beating against her rib cage. Waves of anger emanated from him with a kind of intensity that brought panic into her stomach and all through her chest. It scared her even more than the faceless prowler who had ransacked her apartment.

"L-let me go."

He released her immediately, took a step back, then stood staring at her, his hands at his sides. "I'm sorry,'' he said, not looking away from her face. There was a fleeting ripple in his expression, as if he'd just been told something unexpected. As if he could read her mind . . .

The hair rose along the back of Brooke's neck. She wrapped her hands around her upper arms, where his touch had burned through the cotton sleeves of her T-shirt, and stared at him, unable to look away. There had been something shockingly intimate in that touch. She was too aware of his wide shoulders and muscled chest, of the quiet rasp of his breath as he drew it in, of the faint cotton scent of his shirt, of the fact that he was a man and she was a woman. . . .

"Do you have any idea who could have done this, Brooke?'' he asked levelly.

"I don't know. A burglar, I guess. . . .''

He glanced around the room, to the expensive stereo on top of the cabinet, to a pair of diamond and gold earrings, her high-school graduation gift from her parents, lying on the rug, to the books stacked almost neatly in front of the bookcase.

His black, level gaze moved back to her, fixed on her face with direct purpose. Undefined guilt—and a spark of sensuality that had no place in this encounter—rippled through her. She dismissed it on a wave of guilty, defensive anger. "I don't have any idea who did it,'' she flared at him. "I didn't invite someone to come in here and ransack my apartment!''

"Lum's burned to the ground an hour ago, Brooke. The arson squad's been called in.''

"What?'' Her defenses crumbled like dry sand. She stared at him, stricken, her fragile hold on the events of this night overwhelmed by a surging, frightening flood of images.

Someone had burned down a building. Someone had broken into her apartment. Did Marc Lasaralle think there was a connection? She had been there, yesterday, at Lum's. She had set off the alarm. Did he think—?

The breath went out of her lungs in a rush. He thought she was a suspect. He was questioning her as a suspect in an arson case.

She opened her mouth to speak, but no words came out. She wanted her father. She wanted her father to protect her, to shelter her in the all-engulfing, sometimes smothering protection she'd fought all her life.

What she saw in Marc Lasaralle's eyes was nothing like her father's protective evasion. It was direct, relentless pursuit of the truth.

Four

—

Her voice was a ragged whisper. "I had n-nothing to do with that fire."

Something almost like sympathy flickered in his eyes, but he didn't offer her easy reassurance. "I just want some answers, Brooke."

"But I don't know anything!"

"I think," he said, almost softly, "maybe you do."

She shook her head. "I—"

"What was someone looking for in here?"

"I don't know," she said again. "I don't know what anyone could have wanted."

"Do you keep any money in the apartment, other than what was in your wallet?"

"No."

"Keys? Safety deposit box? Anything like that?"

She shook her head again.

His look swept around the ravaged room. Brooke's eyes followed his. She bent down and reached for the earrings.

"Leave them there," Lasaralle said peremptorily. "Don't touch anything in here until we've had a chance to go over it.'"

She pulled her hands back and wrapped them around herself. "All right," she said in a small voice.

There was something in his look—some personal awareness of her defeated, helpless feelings—that tugged at her in a way she didn't understand. She made herself resist it. Marc Lasaralle wasn't going to protect her. "Is that all?"

"No. What were you doing at that news store yesterday?"

"I told you—it was where my father was shot. I was thinking about him and . . ." She trailed off.

"Your father was shot there three months ago," he said. "Yesterday you set off an alarm designed to detect breaking and entering, then the place burned to the ground. What were you doing there?"

She broke the contact of their gazes with a physical effort and buried her face in her hands, rubbing her fingertips hard against her forehead.

Don't tell Mom. The ridiculous, irrelevant sentence echoed in her mind, carrying all the weight of a childhood commandment. She couldn't betray her father, her family.

But her father had been shot to death. Two people had died. A building had burned. Could there be some awful connection? She didn't know what to do. She couldn't make a decision that difficult. She couldn't.

Her throat made a sound she hadn't willed. She turned, avoiding Marc Lasaralle's eyes, and headed toward the kitchen. Her wine glass, still half-full, was on the table, beside the phone. She gazed at it, unseeing, then she reached out and picked up the phone book.

The logbook page was gone.

Her cry of dismay, unconscious and instinctive, ended any choice. She turned to face Lasaralle, her eyes wide with shock.

"What's missing?" he said abruptly.

Her silence—and the decision she made in it—lasted only a few heartbeats. "My father's logbook," she said, spitting out the words in a rush. "The last page. The night he was killed."

He pulled his hands out of his pockets and straightened his shoulders. "What did it say?"

Brooke made herself meet his gaze. "I can't remember specifically, but...it was filled out for the whole night. He died at 1:00 a.m.," she said. "It shouldn't have been filled out for the night. He...must have had some reason to fill it out in advance."

He stared at her, unblinking, until she turned away. "What else?" he said quietly.

She searched her mind for what else. "It didn't have any reference to Lum's. I guess he didn't expect to be there, maybe, or—" She stopped, but the words were clear in her mind: *He didn't want anyone to know he was there.*

"Who knew you had that page?"

"No one." She met his eyes again and looked down at her hands. "No one." Her hands were shaking. She twisted them together in front of her.

He reached for her. His hold on her shoulders was strong, certain, but it had none of the force he'd used when he'd shaken her at the door. Still, the reaction she felt was the same heady, terrifying mixture of panic and sensual awareness, the same shocking, intimate connection that was all the more shocking because with half her mind she wanted him to touch her, to hold her....

"Somebody knows it now," he said. "I turned in that logbook to headquarters. Somebody knew it."

"I didn't set that fire," she said, her voice husky.

His palms moved fractionally against the skin of her upper arms. The soft cotton of the T-shirt caressed her.

"I know," he said.

His gaze dropped momentarily to her mouth, just long enough for her to know what he was thinking. Her breath caught in her throat, and her heart started to thud. *She couldn't trust him,* she told herself. *She couldn't let herself trust him.*

"Trust your own instincts, Brooke," he said, in a voice that sounded, for all the world, like an answer to her unspoken thoughts.

She started violently and wrenched herself away from him.

He frowned at her, puzzled, and dropped his hands to his sides. He took a deep breath, then glanced away from her, acknowledging her withdrawal. He wouldn't touch her. He wasn't a threat. "The technician will be here before the night's out," he said.

She nodded.

His gaze flicked over her in a half-involuntary sweep. She felt it all the way to her toes.

"You don't have to stay here and wait," he said. "Why don't you let me take you out for breakfast while they go over the place?"

It was a surprising offer from a policeman taking a call. And he hadn't made it, she knew, as a policeman. "No." She shook her head. "I can't. I have to work. I'm meeting a client at nine. I mean—" she gestured vaguely toward her littered desk "—I'll have to make arrangements to meet him. I can't."

They both knew she was babbling. *Don't say it,* she pleaded silently.

He let out a long breath, his gaze on her face until she looked away from him. "Please," she got out. "If you're through here, please leave."

There was a long silence. He hooked his thumbs into the belt loops of his jeans and turned toward the living room. At the doorway he hesitated, then spun back toward her. "Is there someone you can call to stay with you? Someone from your family?"

"No." She shook her head. "No. The landlady's right downstairs. I'll be all right."

"Yeah. Lock the door after me," he told her from the doorway. "I'll wait in the street until there's someone else here."

The door shut softly. Brooke stood in the middle of the room, facing it, trying to summon relief, biting her lip against an errant, crazy feeling that she wanted to call him back.

The station room was hot, cluttered and noisy with the daily business of a major city's police force. Brooke stood just inside the doorway, her briefcase in her hand, scanning the crowded room. She'd been told

Marc Lasaralle wasn't here. She wanted to make sure before she walked in.

Charlie Wilson was at a desk in the far corner—alone. Conscious of relief, Brooke started toward him.

She'd heard nothing about any possible investigation into the arson at Lum's, and no one had told her if she was suspected of having a part in it. Not in words, anyway.

The officer who had come to take prints had asked a few technical questions, done his job and left—with no clear prints to record. The trespasser had worn rubber gloves, he'd told her. It didn't look promising for finding the criminal, but she would be kept informed, he'd added. He hadn't said when.

She caught a few covert glances, a few raised heads, as she threaded her way through the rabbit warren of desks. She ignored the wave of heat in her face. She hadn't been accused of anything. They couldn't know. . . .

"Hey, baby, how ya doing?"

Brooke turned to face the frankly sexy, come-hither grin of a young cop she'd met years ago, when he'd started on the force and she was still in college.

She gave him a wave and skirted his desk, not returning the smile.

There was a good-natured guffaw and a muttered, "Eat your heart out, partner," from the man sitting next to him.

"Don't pay any attention to him, Brooke," one of the other men commented, grinning as she passed him. "You're the best thing he's seen since last month's girlie magazine."

At the mention of her name, Charlie Wilson looked up. He saw her immediately, and she caught surprise and wariness on his face before he stood, dropped his pen on the papers in front of him and glared repressively at the young cop who'd made the last comment.

He didn't turn back to her until she was standing by his desk, and then it was only to give her a curt nod.

"Charlie?" she said. "Are you busy? I mean, could I talk to you for a minute?"

He hesitated long enough to make his reluctance clear. "If you're looking for Marc—"

"No," she said too quickly. She colored. "No, I'm not. I've already talked with him, at my apartment. The night of the break-in."

The older man nodded. "Yeah," he said. "I know."

Brooke gazed at him cautiously, sensing covert curiosity from the men in the room.

"Everyone within earshot of the chief knew it," Charlie went on. "My partner didn't happen to be on duty that night when he took the call."

Brooke swallowed and said, "I didn't ask him to take that call."

Charlie's gaze dropped from hers. He picked up the pen and distractedly tapped the papers on his desk.

"I didn't ask that my apartment be broken into, either."

He still wouldn't look at her.

"Or that somebody burn down that news store. I didn't have anything to do with that!"

He looked up sharply. "Who's saying you did?"

There was a short, charged silence, then the sound of Charlie's exhaled breath. "Oh, geez," he muttered. "Haven't we had enough trouble about this already?"

"I don't want any more trouble. I just want to find out a few things that I—"

"I can't help you, Brooke," he said quietly. "This isn't my investigation."

Brooke watched him, silent for a moment. On his desk was a photograph of a trim blond woman with her arm around a teenager. His family, she guessed. "You knew my father, Charlie. You must have owed him at least one favor. I'm calling it in."

Charlie met her gaze for a long moment while his expression changed from wary reticence to guarded resignation. Finally he dropped the pen on the desk and let out a long sigh. "Have a seat," he said.

Brooke sat on the edge of a chair. "Thanks." Around her, typewriters clicked, file drawers slid on their tracks and the shuffle of daily work filled in the awkward silence. No one seemed to be listening. And even if they were, she couldn't afford to let it matter.

"When I got up this morning, there was a black and white car parked at the end of the street," she said steadily. "Every half hour, yesterday, a patrol car came by."

Charlie's gaze was fixed on his desk, the set of his shoulders unyielding. "There's patrol cars all over the city, Brooke. That's their job. You can't read something into it because they happened to be in your neighborhood."

"Charlie," she said steadily, "I've been a cop's daughter long enough to know extra surveillance when I see it."

Charlie's heavy shoulders slumped. He leaned back in the chair. "Yeah," he said. "I guess you have." He passed a hand down his face and rubbed his jawline with thumb and forefinger. "All right, I'll level with you. My partner asked some of the men to keep an eye on you."

Her stomach tightened. "Am I under investigation, then?"?

Charlie frowned at her. "No. There is no investigation. Marc's just . . . collecting on some favors."

"But I thought on the fire at Lum's, the arson squad had been called in. I thought they were investigating for arson."

"This has nothing to do with Lum's."

"Is that what Sergeant Lasaralle thinks? Is that what he told the arson squad?"

Charlie let out a heavy sigh. "Look, the arson unit might have been called in, they might suspect that someone set that fire, might even be able to prove it, but that doesn't give 'em any real leads." He leaned forward. "Arsonists are hard to catch. That fire could have been set by the owner himself, looking for an insurance payoff. Could've been some guy with a grudge against the business. Could've been kids. It's pretty hard to prove anything at all in a case like that. And they've got a dozen more sitting on their desks waiting to be solved. This thing hasn't got any more priority than any of the others." He glanced at her. "And as far as I'm concerned—as far as anybody is concerned—it's got nothing to do with you."

Brooke stared at him, wanting to accept the words at face value. It could well be true. The arson could have no connection to her father. She could just go home, forget all this, pretend it never happened....

"So why am I being tailed?" she asked, her voice tinged with a kind of challenge she hadn't consciously put into it.

This time, Charlie didn't look away from her. "Because...after the break-in...my partner wanted someone to watch out for you."

She felt a curl of fear in her midsection. "But why?" Her fingers tightened convulsively on the soft leather of her briefcase. "Why do I need protection from a routine burglary that got stopped as soon as they found out I was home? They didn't even take much of anything. I'm not in any danger!" Her voice had risen. She could hear the shrill note of panic, and see gazes flick in her direction. She bit her lip, self-conscious.

"Look," Charlie said cautiously, "Marc gets... hunches, sometimes."

She felt the skin along her arms prickle. "Psychic premonitions, you mean."

Charlie's gaze dropped. "I don't—"

"He had some kind of hunch that something's going to happen—or that I'm involved in something?"

Charlie exhaled a short breath.

"What?" Brooke asked sharply.

The older man ran his hand down his face again. "He's a good cop, Brooke. He's being careful. He just doesn't want to take any chances."

"I don't need protection," she said shakily.

"Maybe not. Maybe you don't. Not everyone who gets protection is really threatened."

"No," she said evenly. "Sometimes the person getting the 'protection' is a suspect."

He leaned across the desk toward her, lowering his voice. There was a flicker of sympathy in his expression. "What do you have to be suspected of, Brooke? You kept your father's logbook. You tore out a page. Yeah—" he nodded at the involuntary sound she made "—I know about that. Marc mentioned it."

"Then he must have mentioned that it was filled out for the night my father died. In advance."

"So it was filled out for the night. What does that prove? He was probably just saving time on the paperwork, same's we all do now and again."

"But the page was taken. Marc—" She swallowed. "Sergeant Lasaralle thought somebody knew about it."

Charlie frowned. "Who could have known it? Marc didn't even know it." He shook his head. "Forget about it, Brooke. It doesn't mean anything. Stop worrying."

Brooke fell silent. *Forget about it. Stop worrying.* Charlie's kindly paternalism wrapped around her like a blanket she'd owned since childhood, familiar, habitual, lulling her with the promise of security and protection. It was a promise she'd been brought up to believe in, never to doubt, never to question....

"You sound like my father," she said, with a wan smile. "'Don't worry. I'll take care of it.' He wanted us to think nothing would ever happen that he couldn't take care of." She let out a long breath. "Now my mother can't even change a fuse."

Charlie made a small gesture with his hand of understanding and sympathy. "You know if she needs help, anyone on the force would be there, Brooke."

She nodded. "Charlie," she asked, around a sudden lump in her throat, "was my father a good cop?"

Charlie met her steady gaze. "I would have said so. I would have said there wasn't any better."

It wasn't quite a *yes*, but it was, she knew, all Charlie could say in honesty. Brooke looked down at her lap. "My brother's a rookie, in the police academy this year. Pop was his hero. He needs to believe that."

"Yeah. Of course he does. And there's no reason why he shouldn't, is there?"

She glanced up at him.

"Nobody's gonna open any investigations because of a page out of a patrol log," he said. "Even if it turns up. And that's not reason enough for you to start inventing trouble, either," he added. "Or start questioning things you know nothing about."

She bit her lip, feeling disloyal, thinking of Billy, her mother....

Charlie could be right. All this could have nothing to do with her father. Nothing to do with her.

Or maybe it could.

Neither Charlie Wilson nor Marc Lasaralle knew about the five thousand dollars in an unmarked envelope in her father's desk drawer. No one knew about it. No one but— Her hands clenched around her briefcase as a tiny piece of the puzzle clicked into place. She knew, suddenly, what someone might have been looking for in her apartment. The money.

She grasped the edge of her chair and slid out of it. It was time to leave. She had to get out of this station room, away from the desks and typewriters and the atmosphere of stark, hard facts and the dangerous implications of the fact she had just recognized. She knew, in the back of her mind, what it meant: that she herself was inextricably tangled in this—whatever it was. She couldn't face that right now.

"Charlie, thank you," she got out.

He stood. "Don't worry, Brooke," Charlie told her. "Marc won't let anything happen to you."

Her stomach was clenched into a knot, and her palms were clammy, but from somewhere she summoned a smile and a gesture of appreciation. There was some horrible irony in Charlie's reassurance. Marc Lasaralle wouldn't let anything happen to her— except the consequences of relentless truth and unvarnished reality.

Marc Lasaralle *was* what she was afraid of. He was the link to all the things she didn't want to face, all the hard realities she wasn't sure she had the courage for.

She turned, drew in a breath and willed herself to walk steadily across the room. She made it without looking at anyone—to the lobby, past the desk, across the floor toward the door.

Then Marc Lasaralle walked through it and stopped squarely in front of her, his black eyes fixed on hers as if he could see every thought in her mind.

Five

―――

"Sergeant Lasaralle." Brooke's tone of voice was an attempt at normalcy. It didn't work.

Marc Lasaralle's dark, direct gaze took her in with one swift pass.

"Ms. Shelburne. What are you doing here?"

"I'm picking up some press releases."

His eyes narrowed. "No more trouble at your apartment?"

"No! No, there hasn't been any more trouble at my apartment." She should leave it at that, she knew. But he was standing too close, and she made the mistake of meeting his arrogant, too-knowing glance. Her temper snapped. "As I'm sure you already know, *Sergeant*!"

"If I knew it, I wouldn't have asked."

"If you don't know it, then what's the point of having me tailed?"

There was a short, charged silence, barely intruded upon by the self-conscious indifference of the two men at the front desk and the duty officer filling out a stack of reports.

"Maybe," Marc Lasaralle said, "we could discuss this privately." He took her by the elbow, walked her half a dozen steps down the hallway, then reached in front of her to open the door to a tiny room. He held the door open, waiting for her to walk through it.

Brooke swiftly took in the scarred wooden table, the two mismatched chairs, the overhead fan. An interrogation room.

She forced herself to face him. "All right," she told him, a touch of defiance in her voice. "I'll listen while you discuss it." She brushed past him inside, and Marc let the door swing shut behind them. The working sounds of the police station dimmed.

He crossed to the half-opened window with two strides and stood staring out for a moment, his back to her. He was wearing a white, short-sleeved baseball jersey that stretched tautly across his shoulders and his lean waist. He didn't have his gun, but she didn't have any trouble picturing him with it. The casual, kid-in-college shirt didn't conceal the mature width of his shoulders or the taut muscles of his upper arms. His chinos were pleated at the waist, unironed and loose, but the muscled strength of his thighs was explicitly suggested in the way he stood, weight on one hip, feet widespread on the worn linoleum floor. The masculine power in that superbly toned and taut body was undeniable. Without warning, she felt the vagrant urge to run her hands along his shoulders, to trace the ridges of his strong back. Brooke clenched her fingers around her briefcase.

He turned to face her. "You're being tailed for your own protection, Brooke."

The flat declaration, frightening in its implications, slapped at her like cold water. "I don't need protection!" She hugged her briefcase to her chest in a gesture that unconsciously contradicted her words. "There's been no more trouble on my street since the break-in."

"Good. That's what the surveillance is there for. To prevent trouble."

"Well, then, they'll be happy to hear that their efforts have protected all my ashtrays and every penny of the fifteen dollars in my wallet."

His arrogant stance didn't change, but a muscle tightened at the side of his jaw. "There's more to this than a routine burglary, Brooke. We both know that."

"I don't know that! I don't know anything like that! I told you everything I knew two days ago."

"And what about now?" he said levelly.

The uncanny perception jolted her. A prickle of superstition raised the hair on the back of her neck. "You're the one who called out the undercover police surveillance, Sergeant. What is it *you're* not telling *me*?"

She knew she shouldn't have said it the moment the words were out of her mouth. It was a mistake to pit herself against Marc Lasaralle on any level. So why had she?

The answer came as quickly as the question. To back off would be to admit that because she was afraid of him, she would let Marc Lasaralle walk into her life and rearrange it in whatever way he saw fit. Just the way her mother had let her life be ordered and arranged....

He slowly straightened. "Okay, I'll tell you what I know."

There was an unspoken challenge in the statement, which made her pulse quicken. Brooke stared at him mutely.

"I know your father was killed in a police action in Lum's parking lot three months ago. The man who shot him—and who died there with him—was a professional. He did breaking and enterings for a price, and he didn't keep job notes, but we know he was local. And he was good. He didn't get caught by accident."

Brooke swallowed convulsively, but Marc Lasaralle's level gaze didn't leave her face.

"I know you haven't had that logbook ever since he died, Brooke. The department made some routine inquiries for it. Your name was listed as the family member who insisted they follow up on the search. Nobody had it."

She felt heat in her face, but at the same time a chill ran down her spine. "I . . . I didn't . . ."

"So it must have been there at Lum's," he went on. "It must have been somewhere at the site of that building. You must have set off that alarm while you were searching for it."

The scene in front of her shifted in an odd, disturbing way. She felt transparent, as though the man standing in front of her could see through flesh and bone to the depths of her soul. The sense of violation was just as shocking as when he'd searched her in the parking lot at Lum's. And her own reaction to it was just as inexplicable. She felt a warm, faint stirring, as confusing as the seesawing between the familiarity and resentment she felt for the station house they were in. As confusing as her conflicting impulses between defiant truth and the need to protect her family.

"All right," she said, her voice ragged. "I did find it there. I knew it had to be there somewhere. He...always carried it."

He acknowledged her confession with a few seconds' silence. Through the half-open window behind him, a breath of hot air, scented with sun-dried juniper and exhaust fumes, rippled his jersey. He said, "Somebody who had an interest knew you found it. I turned it in to the front desk that afternoon. Anybody who knew that, or who just happened to be in the right place, could have taken a look at it. And that night your apartment was burglarized."

"That doesn't prove anything! Apartments in Hartford are burglarized all the time! It could have been just coincidence."

"Yeah. It could have been." The words were steady, cold and unconvinced. "I also know," he went on relentlessly, "how long you've been doing PR work for the police department. Three months. Before that you worked on the campaign staff of Senator Albert Andrews."

She drew in a sharp breath. "What right do you have to investigate me?"

"You were fired shortly before your father's death. For no reason that sounded convincing to me."

"He was overstaffed!"

"By one?"

"I don't know! Maybe he just didn't like my work. Or my politics. Or something. I don't know!"

"Neither do I." He slid his hands into his pockets. "Maybe we can find out."

The "we" was somehow more threatening than the litany of his interrogation. She couldn't give him her cooperation—not in this, and not in anything else. She wasn't willing to risk destroying her father's reputation, her brother's hero-worship, her mother's fragile acceptance of the tragedy in their lives. "I don't want to find out."

"Why not?"

"I want you to leave it alone. Stop investigating me. And stop having my apartment watched, and just drop the whole thing. Leave it alone. Leave *me* alone!"

His eyes narrowed. "And just pretend that everyone else is going to leave you alone, too? Like they did the other nght?"

"I—I don't need—"

"Yes, you do, Brooke. You think you can make this all go away by pretending it doesn't exist? You think if I call off the watchdogs you'll be safer without them?"

Yes, she did. She knew it was an illusory safety. She knew it wasn't based on hard truth. And maybe she couldn't maintain it. But she couldn't bring herself to let go of an illusion that protected all of them—her mother, her brother, her own childhood beliefs.

"That's an illusion you can't afford, Brooke."

She made a small, startled, unintentional sound in the back of her throat. He had done it again—answered her thoughts. And she didn't like it. She didn't like the shiver that went down her spine every time she thought of the word that described his strange, uncanny sense. She didn't like the way he looked at her without blinking or glancing away—as if he could see through her words into the thoughts behind them, as if she had whispered all her most intimate secrets to him in the warm darkness of a shared night. She didn't like knowing he had run his palms along the sides of her body. And most of all, she realized with an appalling jolt of insight, she didn't like the way he made her wonder what it would feel like if he did it again.

Still clutching her briefcase to her chest, she took a step back and started to turn away from him, toward the door.

He reached toward her, caught her wrist in his fingers, and stopped her. "You can't afford *any* illusions, Brooke." His touch was gentle, a light, casual emphasis to his point, but there was nothing casual about her reaction to it. She felt it in every nerve of her body, as if the connection were as solid as a steel handcuff, or a kiss.

She was aware of the sensation of heat—the hot, barely moving air from the ceiling fan, the dusty smell of old wood in the humid air, the glare of sun slanting onto the linoleum floor through the window, the warmth that radiated from her body as if she herself had absorbed the hot, relentless energy of that midsummer sun.

"You went to that parking lot because you wanted to find out what really happened, didn't you?" he said. "You think your father was on the take, and you have to know if it's true."

"No." It was an unconvincing whisper. And she didn't know herself if the denial was aimed at his words or at the crazy racing of her pulse and the sensual flutter in her stomach.

"Now you're up to your neck in something you can't handle alone." His voice dropped to a gruff, husky murmur that stirred her nerve endings like cool water over a sandy ledge. "You need protection, Brooke, and I'm not going to let up on it until you're safe again."

He was close enough so that she could see the pulse beating in the hollow of his throat, above the loose neck of the white jersey. The personal, intimate summer smell of washed cotton over heated skin permeated her consciousness.

"It wasn't even your case," she told him, breathless.

"No." The agreement was low, rough, and unsettling. "It wasn't my case."

"Then why..." Her question trailed off into the hot soughing of the air in the bushes outside the window.

"You know why." He moved an inch closer to her, compelling her toward him with a gentle touch on the wrist he'd moved from her briefcase, and a slow, almost unconscious caress of his thumb against her pulse point. Her blood heated into uncontrolled response as he bent toward her, his head tipped to one side, blotting out the glare of the window behind him as his lips neared hers.

"Don't," she said just before their lips touched. She turned aside, raising her briefcase closer to her face with one hand, trying to put a barrier between them, though there was no suggestion of force in the light, seductive grip on her wrist.

His thumb continued the small caress. "Why not? You can't say you haven't thought about it."

She let out her pent up breath in a rush. "I don't want you to know what I think about!" She tugged against his hand. It was a small, desperate movement, but he released her immediately. The absence of his touch disoriented her for a moment. She wrapped her free hand around the briefcase to keep from wanting him to touch her again. "That's just it," she said in a rush. "I don't want you to know what I think. I don't want you in my mind."

"I don't want to read your mind, Brooke. I just want to kiss you." His breath was coming just as fast as her own.

"How do I know it's not the same thing?"

"Why don't you let me try it? Then we'll both know." His hand rose to the hair on her shoulder. Not touching her skin, he brushed it back. Again her eyes met his intense gaze. "I've thought about this since the first time I saw you in front of that building, with your hair loose like this, and that look on your face, like you weren't going to give in to anybody. I've been thinking about it ever since." He was so close his breath fanned her cheek and the husky murmur of his voice vibrated in her ear like the first faint intimate caress. "It's like the hunches I get sometimes. I don't seem to have any control over it. Telling myself I'm a cop and you don't want anything to do with cops doesn't seem to make any difference. I don't know if anything about you or me makes a difference. I just know I can't shut it off. I just know I have to do this...."

His fingers twined into the hair at the nape of her neck, cool against her heated skin, and he lowered his mouth the remaining fraction of an inch and brought his lips to hers. The touch was light, gentle. His free hand brushed her shoulder with a stroke that was feather-light, sensitive, slow. As if with that barest contact he could hold her there, make her want to accept his kiss....

Brooke's eyes slid closed as the urge to resist him evaporated like water on hot pavement, and the wish to escape gave way to something sweet and unexplored deep inside her. He drew her toward him as his mouth lingered over hers, and her arms, still wrapped around the briefcase, were pressed into his chest.

When she made no effort to turn away from him, he gently, slowly tipped her head by slow, inexorable degrees to fit their mouths together. He slid an arm across her shoulder blades to the center of her back and tightened his hold, pulling her against him, as if it were her breasts, and not her briefcase, flattened against his muscular chest.

She felt the warm, wet tip of his tongue flick along the closed line of her lips. He moved his mouth, nudging, slanting, exploring their union.

The torn loyalty in her mind, the anxious fretting about her family, her father's memory, her own questions, all dissipated into the warmth of the summer afternoon. The sweet, melting honey of sensuality flowed through her as she leaned against him and tipped her head back into his hand. She let her lips part at the prodding of his tongue, and the warm, sensuous invasion set her heart thrumming in her ears and her pulse racing in response.

His hold tightened, urging her closer, as if in a plea for her to tighten her own embrace. The pressure of his kiss increased as his tongue slid along the sensitive inner surface of her lips and his mouth widened to encircle hers possessively. She drifted under his spell, wholly surrendered to it, lost in sensation as sweet awareness unfurled inside her. Her briefcase was still crushed between them, keeping their bodies apart, but in Brooke's mind an image formed of herself and Marc, wrapped in an embrace as hot as the mysterious darkness that seemed to surround them, as intoxicating as the sharp, pungent herb that scented the air. He was shirtless; she was dressed in nothing but some thin, diaphanous wisp of a garment, and she could feel his body along the whole length of hers. Her breasts were crushed against the hard, defined muscle of his chest, her nipples rigid and sensitized; her stomach was flat against his hips. The ridge of aroused male flesh pressed against her intimately, and her arms were around him, palms flat on damp, warm bare skin heated by the burning glow of the fire that surrounded them like a circle of flame in some savage pagan ritual.

They were lovers ordained by that ritual, man and woman in that ancient, overpowering circle of fire and earth. They were locked together in a savage, beautiful, inexorable mating of man and woman, where choice and will had no power against the unchained forces of fire and fertility.

Brooke felt Marc's hands tense, as if in startled reaction to the wild image in her mind. His hands gripped her shoulders, tightened momentarily, then gently, deliberately, pushed her away from him as he lifted his mouth from hers and drew in a quick, audible breath.

Her hold on the briefcase slackened. Marc caught it as it slipped from her hands, but his gaze stayed fixed on hers. He let out the breath he'd sucked in, and tightened his hands around the soft leather as if he didn't trust himself not to drop it. His eyes closed momentarily, and she saw him swallow before he murmured, "My God..."

Brooke folded her shaky arms in front of her. She hugged her elbows, trying to chase the chill that quickly washed over her at the absence of his lips on hers, his arms around her. She slid her hands up to her shoulders, willing her body not to want him, willing her mind away from that erotic image....

But she did want him, almost unbearably. His dark eyes watched her with bemused intensity. His lips were slightly open as he drew in another breath, revealing just the edge of his chipped tooth. What would it have felt like if she'd run her tongue over it, met his kiss with her own bold exploration?

"Brooke," he said, his voice a gruff, low murmur. "That dream...the fire..."

She stiffened as the image of their bodies twined together flashed into her mind again. It hadn't, she realized with a disorienting jolt, been conjured by her alone. It was Marc's fantasy. She knew instinctively. There was something compellingly masculine about that scene, something essentially male in the ritual of desire, danger, primitive possession. It was a dream that belonged in the world of violence and danger that

Marc Lasaralle inhabited. Marc's fantasy. Somehow he had sent it into her mind, into the very fabric of her soul...

Why don't you let me try it? Then we'll both know, he'd said.

Brooke made a strangled sound as her lungs pulled in air and her feet finally moved to take a stumbling step away from him.

She didn't want to know this. She didn't want to risk her loyalty, her damaging secrets, her will to resist.

Without speaking, without any gesture of good-bye, she rammed her hands into her pockets, closed her fingers around her car keys, then turned and fled out the door of the hot room and across the lobby of the police station.

Marc didn't try to stop her. He stood where he was in the stifling heat of the tiny room, watching the door bang shut after her. She was fleeing from something his strange gift told him she couldn't escape.

No more than he could. He'd lived most of his life knowing that he was different, knowing that he was marked irrevocably by a gift that was sometimes as much a curse as an asset. Yet he'd been shaken by the powerful compulsion of that kiss... by the flash of dream that he *knew*, without questioning how, that she had shared.

He didn't know what it meant. But he was sure beyond a shadow of a doubt that sooner or later they would both have to find out. The heat that flared between them whenever they were within touching distance was a part of something that would draw them in beyond any resistance. And what they were being drawn into would have to be faced—the truth, the lies, the still hidden criminal purposes that had set these events in motion, the present danger that he knew threatened Brooke Shelburne as surely as he knew his badge number.

At the thought of Brooke coming to harm, Marc's fingers tightened on the leather briefcase. He glanced down at it, realizing belatedly what it was. She'd left him holding her briefcase.

He pushed open the door, sprinted across the lobby and dashed out to the stone steps at the front of the station. The taillights of Brooke's car were just disappearing around the corner at the end of the street.

Six

Marc knew she didn't want him to return it. He'd guessed that reaction even before he'd called her and offered to bring the briefcase to her apartment. She'd pick it up herself, she'd told him.

Marc felt a muscle in his jaw clench at the unspoken rebuff. She didn't want him in her apartment. What did she think he was going to do? Sweep her off her feet and carry her into the bedroom he'd glimpsed the other night? Settle them both down on that lacy Victorian bedspread, unzip his pants and smooth her skirt up to her waist, and fit himself into that dark feminine nest of velvet heat....

A groan worked its way to the back of his throat. That was what he'd wanted to do this afternoon. He'd wanted it so badly that he'd conjured up that strange, compelling dream that had started the night he'd met her. And for a moment, Brooke had felt it, too. When she'd returned his kiss...

At the thought of her brief, sweet surrender he could feel himself growing hard and hot, the wave of heat licking through him like a flame.

God, if they'd been anywhere but an interrogation room in the police station...

His mouth quirked.

Yeah, sure. And if he were anything but a cop, and she were anything but a cop's daughter up to her neck in some kind of trouble...

There was a warning itch at the base of his skull. He *knew* she was in trouble. Police trouble. It didn't matter that he himself was convinced of her innocence. She was a possible suspect in an arson case. And he was crazy as hell to even consider getting involved with her. It went against all the rules of investigative police work, against all common sense and objective reasoning.

The problem was his body didn't know that.

He shut his eyes, shoved his hands deep into his pockets and tried hard to forget what his body was telling him.

Behind his closed eyelids he saw a quick vision of the dream that wouldn't let him go: Brooke's soft, sweet body pressed against his, nothing between them but folds of cloth so gossamer-thin he could feel the texture of her skin beneath it—her flat stomach, the lush curves of her breasts, the nipples gathered into tight little knots, ready for the touch of his hands, the hot, wet stroking of his tongue...

Marc opened his eyes, ripped his hands out of his pockets and stared without seeing at the blank television in the corner of the living room.

Forget it, he told himself.

He crossed to the kitchen counter, got out the scotch and made himself a drink. The drink wouldn't help—he knew it—but the act of pouring it was marginally distracting. He brought the glass back to the couch and sat down beside Brooke's briefcase. He set the drink on the coffee table, stared sourly at the brown leather satchel, then stifled a brief protest from his conscience and reached over to flip up the cover.

Inside was a thin sheaf of papers—press releases for the police department drug education drive, official announcements of promotions and awards for the month of July, a news release.

Incumbent State Senator Albert Andrews, in an informal visit to the central station of Hartford Police Headquarters, urged the department to step up its investigation of illegal gambling activities in the city. The senator, running on a clean government platform, opposes budget cuts for police and firefighters in the district and supports police efforts...

Marc frowned at the press release. There was a nagging, itch-under-the-skin feeling about it that bothered him. He remembered the visit, a predictable campaign stop for the smooth, savvy, clean-image politician who knew what was needed to further his public ambitions. The press release Brooke had typed up was routine: polished and carefully slanted to flatter both the department and the senator. As it was supposed to do.

She was obviously good at her job. She had a way with glossy phrases, public images and polite evasions. The uncloaked passion he'd glimpsed for a few tantalizing moments in the interrogation room was a thing she kept under tight wraps, under layers of evasion.

He felt his jaw clench. Brooke hadn't lied to him outright. He would have sensed it if she had. But she wasn't leveling with him, either.

And he wasn't enough of a psychic to figure her out—or to figure out what was bothering him about Albert Andrews. She'd worked for the man until three months ago. Then she'd been fired, for no good reason.

Frowning, he shoved the paper back into the briefcase.

She wasn't leveling with him. And what that fact should tell him was that he shouldn't get emotionally involved with her....

Angry with himself, his situation and the world in general, Marc snapped the briefcase shut, reached for the TV and turned on the ball game. It wasn't going to make any difference when Brooke Shelburne came to get her press releases. There wasn't any point in watching the clock.

An hour and seventeen minutes later the lights of her car turned into his driveway. It took forty-seven seconds for the doorbell to buzz.

Ten seconds later he opened the door to find her poised sideways, studying the shrubbery beside his front porch. She spun around, taken by surprise, and pushed her hands into the pockets of loose, baggy jeans. An untucked orange T-shirt hung to her hips. Marc felt something tighten in his stomach at the sight of her.

They stood looking at each other for a long, self-conscious moment of mutual appraisal. The sun, lowering in the early evening sky but still warm as melting butter, splayed over the back of Brooke's neck and shoulders.

She cleared her throat. "Hi." Her voice was a thin squeak. She swallowed and tried again. "You're home."

"Yes. I said I'd be." Marc stepped back from the door and opened it wide. "Come on in."

"I really just came for the briefcase," she said quickly.

"I know. It's inside."

She hesitated, glancing past his shoulder to glimpse polished floors with no rugs, wood-framed windows bare of curtains, the edge of a black and white photograph. She shouldn't go in. She knew that. But she couldn't help feeling curious about his house. "You could have left it at the station. I mean I hope you didn't go to any trouble."

"No. No trouble."

He stood waiting, the door open. Behind him in the living room, a TV broadcasted the muted sounds of a ball game. A couch—with her briefcase on it—faced a wall of cabinets, flanked by a low table and one easy chair. That seemed to be the extent of the furnishings.

She stepped over the threshold and walked into the big, starkly appointed room. Her eyes flicked over the bare floor, the monastically clean walls, a lot of empty space decorated with only a section of bookcases and two large photographs.

His voice broke in on her assessment. "I like things plain and simple," he said.

"Yes. I guess you do." She glanced toward him. Their eyes met, and that swift, brief contact sent her temperature up as if he'd caressed her. Marc let go of the door and let it swing shut.

She was alone with him in his house. *Well, so what, Shelburne? You came here to prove you're not interested, didn't you?*

Fighting the irrational emotions that weren't proving anything of the kind, she clasped her hands behind her back and turned away from him to study the photographs on the opposite wall.

One was a black and white picture of a farmhouse kitchen where glass jars of tomatoes lined window-sills, and salmon fillets were spread on a rack in the sunlight from the open window. The other showed a rambling Norman-style stone farmhouse in a rural landscape. The house and buildings were in need of repair, but everywhere in the yard were signs of vigorous life—chickens in front of the flower gardens, laundry flapping on the line, a spinning wheel and an enormous basket of yarn set up outside the front door, where a sleek white cat dozed on the stone step.

"Do you like them?"

At his question she jumped, then turned to find him studying her the way she had been studying the photographs. She felt heat flush her face, unclasped her hands, then clasped them again in front of her. "Yes. They're really..." She trailed off, unable, in the awkward moment, to express her admiration. Brooke bit her lip. *What was the matter with her? She sounded like a tongue-tied seventh grader!* She searched her disordered brain for something intelligent to say. "Were they both done by the same photographer?"

"Yes. My mother."

"Your mother?" Her voice pinched off the last word with surprise.

He nodded. "They're portraits, really, of my grandmother."

"Portraits?" Intrigued at the description, Brooke turned back to the photographs and studied them again. They were, indeed, "portraits," each one stamped with a sense of personality and presence that spoke of the talent of the photographer as well as the distinctiveness of the subject. "She must have been an extraordinary woman," Brooke said. "Your mother, I mean."

"She was. They both were. I come from a long line of extraordinary women."

Brooke glanced at him, tongue-tied again. She had no answer for that statement. She herself came from no such line. She came from a long line of dependent, fragile clinging vines. Women who couldn't so much as . . . retrieve a set of press releases without stammering and blushing and betraying nervousness with every sentence. She squeezed her eyes shut for a moment, trying to gather her composure. She couldn't let herself be like that. She'd stepped out of the protective shell of her family the day she'd gone to that parking lot and found her father's logbook. She'd made her choice. Now she had to live with it.

She drew in a deep breath. "Well, thank you again for bringing home my briefcase. I'll just take it off your hands and be on my way."

His eyebrows rose at the sudden brusqueness in her voice, but he said, without hesitation, "Sure." He crossed the bare floor, picked up the leather case and brought it to her.

She gave a huff of strained laughter. "I can't believe I forgot this. It must have been—"

"The heat?"

Not looking at him, she shrugged awkwardly.

"Yeah," he said after a deliberate pause. "It got pretty hot in that room."

Her startled gaze flew up to his and deep color suffused her face. "That . . . isn't what I meant."

"That's what happened, though," he said, his gaze fixed on her face. "That's why you forgot your papers. Things got so hot that we were tangled up in the same fantasy, and that was just too strange for you, so now you're going to pretend it never happened."

She set her jaw and met his gaze, ignoring the wash of color in her face, welcoming the flush of anger that brought it there. "What do you want me to say? That it wasn't strange? That it's perfectly normal to have someone or something else take over your mind? That it's just an average, everyday occurrence to not be able to control what you think or—" her voice stuck on the phrase "—or feel?"

"No, I don't—"

"Well, I can't say that! It's not normal! I don't want to have any psychic experiences. I never gave you permission to do that!"

"I never gave anybody permission for it, either," he said.

She stared back at him, clutching her briefcase in front of her in an unconscious repetition of her defensive stance that afternoon in the interrogation room.

"My God, Brooke! Do you think I did that on purpose?"

Her grip on the briefcase tightened. "Did you?"

He let out a long, defeated breath before he shook his head. "No. Even if I could have, do you think I would?"

She gave him no answer, hesitating over a strained silence, for it seemed the admission that she trusted him would betray feelings that she needed desperately to keep hidden. The baseball game in the background droned on.

Marc's shoulders slumped. His head fell forward and he hooked one hand over the back of his neck, rubbing at the tensed muscles in a gesture she'd seen him make before.

She caught her lip between her teeth, fighting the urge to believe him, to trust him, to give in to the turmoil of emotion gathering in her mind. *But she couldn't.* He was a cop, and she had something to hide. He wasn't going to protect her and take care of her the way her father had.

"I don't have any more control over it than you do, Brooke. It just happens. I never asked for this. And I never got anything quite so intense, not even when I was—" He hesitated, searching her face.

"Not even when what?" she got out through the tight, strained muscles of her throat.

"There was a woman I was involved with a couple of years ago. I almost married her. But nothing like this ever happened then."

By degrees, she lowered the briefcase until it dangled loosely in front of her hips. "What happened to her?" she asked.

He said, unsmiling, "She thought I was a little too strange. She didn't want to have psychic children."

"Oh." She clicked her tongue in dismay. Against her will she could feel her guard crumbling. What must it be like to live with some trait that set you apart, that made even people you cared about wary and afraid? Yet he hadn't denied it, hadn't pretended to be someone else. Hadn't tried to hide his feelings, as she was trying...

"I'm...sorry," she said.

He nodded. "Yeah. So was I."

Silence stretched between them, filled with the muted sounds of the ball game. The pitcher struck someone out. The roar of the crowd rose in excitement.

He took two steps toward the television, clicked it off, then straightened, turning back to her. "Would you like a drink?" he asked.

The small shake of her head was a quick automatic protest. "No. I...really should..."

"Soda then? A cup of coffee? Cold pizza?" His mouth curved in a characteristic, wry smile. "Ten minutes' conversation?"

It was impossible not to return that smile, not to acknowledge that she wanted to stay, that she wondered even now what his kitchen was like, whether he made his own coffee, what he did in his hours off....

And ten minutes seemed an innocent indulgence. "All right. Coffee."

His smile faded into pensive seriousness at her consent. He gave her a short, single nod, turned and walked into the kitchen.

Brooke watched his retreating back, feeling a momentary, unguarded sense of possibilities. With a final glance around the living room, she set her briefcase down on the coffee table and followed him.

An enormous, scruffy, bobtailed cat raised himself from the counter, back arched in a stretch, then leaped down and sauntered toward the living room, rubbing himself against Brooke's leg as he passed her. Marc grinned. "That's Tarzan. He moved in after I rescued him from a couple of neighborhood dogs. Now I can't get rid of him."

"Have you tried?"

"Nope."

She'd known that would be the answer. She smiled faintly, scanning the room, thinking of what it could tell her of the man who inhabited it. It gave the impression of wood-polished floors, butcher-block counters, wooden cabinets with round wooden knobs. The white porcelain sink, refrigerator and stove, also white, looked comfortably battered enough to have come with the house.

Marc filled a kettle with water, put it on the stove and got out filters and a funnel for a small glass coffeepot sitting on the counter beside the stove.

She crossed to the counter and ran the palm of her hand over the satin-smooth surface and the perfectly squared corner.

"Regular or decaf?" he asked, turning around.

She pulled her hand back as if she'd been touching forbidden treasure, and pushed it deep into her pocket. "Regular's fine."

"Regular it is."

He turned back to the stove, and Brooke's gaze wandered again. A chipped, bright blue cookie jar stood on the counter beneath the cabinets. Early evening sunlight slanted in through the window and glinted on glass jars of home-canned tomatoes. Her glance caught on the bright red jars, then lingered appraisingly, before she leaned one hip against the counter and watched him. His movements were as direct and unselfconscious as the arrogant cat's. With one finger he hooked up the ring of a coffee scoop hanging over the stove, measured out coffee, then flipped it back on its peg. Beneath his white baseball jersey, slightly wrinkled where he had leaned against the couch, his muscles flexed. The neck of the jersey, stretched out wider than it should have been, gaped away from the strong, tanned cords of his neck.

He snapped the lid back on the coffee can and reached with one arm to open a cabinet door, slide the can inside and shut the cabinet again. Brooke's eyes lingered on the bare length of his forearm, drifting over the undeniably masculine texture of tanned skin and dark hair. The ridges of muscle moved with every movement of his hand, every flex of tanned, strong fingers. Mentally she placed her own hand over his, traced the bones of his knuckles, the back of his hand, the sinew and bone of his wrist, where the dark, silky hair of his forearm started. She knew what it would feel like under her palm—the tendons of his forearm, the smooth skin, warmer under his sleeve if she slipped

"Are they from your grandmother?"

"Yes."

Yes. They could have been the jars in the photograph of his grandmother's house. Her hands tightened on the mug. "When you said she was an extraordinary woman..." she hesitated, staring down into the coffee. "Did you mean she was psychic?"

"Yes."

In the warmth of the early morning evening, she felt a chill snake down her spine. "And your mother?"

"Not so much."

"How much is not so much?"

A muscle twitched at the corner of his eye at her too-direct question, and his mouth tightened. She thought for a moment he was going to tell her it was none of her business, but instead he just studied her with that steady gaze, and when he started to speak, his voice was measured, as if he were choosing his words carefully. "My father walked out when I was two. My mom went to work as a legal secretary in a law firm where it's not acceptable for the secretaries to know more than they're told. I have a feeling it wasn't acceptable to my father, either. She's never talked about it."

"Oh." She fell silent for a moment. "I'm sorry. I don't have a right to pry into your life."

"Oh, I don't know. Maybe you do." His lips curved in a brief smile.

"No, I don't," she said too quickly.

"I don't mind, Brooke."

"Your mother might."

"Why?"

"Because..." She gestured, half at a loss to explain a reaction she knew was too dangerously personal. "It must have been hard for her, being left alone like that. She had a baby to take care of, she was practically a widow, left on her own... and she probably didn't expect her husband to just... not be there one day."

"She did what she had to do. She put her life together." In the quiet of the kitchen his voice was low and as intimate as a lover's touch. "Your mother will, too. Brooke. She'll be all right."

Brooke straightened, feeling her shoulder tense. "Don't do that." The words came out in a tight, strained voice.

"Don't do what?"

"Don't read my mind." She put her coffee cup down on the counter and moved a step away from him.

He let out a huff of disbelief. "I wasn't reading your mind!"

"You knew I was thinking about my mother."

"Anybody would have known that." He closed the distance between them with two steps, and when she would have turned away from him, he stopped her with a hand on her elbow. "Anybody paying the least bit of attention would know you're concerned about her, that you worry about whether she can handle everything alone. You wish you could do something to help her, and it hurts you that you can't." His free hand circled her other elbow to keep her turned toward him. "You think I can't know how you feel about your mother without reading your mind?"

"You *don't* know!"

The scrutiny of that dark, direct gaze silenced any further protest she would have spoken. "So tell me," Marc said softly.

She shouldn't tell him. She knew she shouldn't. She should brush him off, tell him something meaningless.

But the glib answer wouldn't come. She swallowed as her throat constricted. "My mother...isn't like yours," she said, her voice raspy. "She's not a strong woman. She can't just pick up the pieces and go on." Her eyes squeezed shut. "She worshipped my father. If she ever found out I was in trouble with the police, she'd fall apart. And my brother—he's in the police academy—"

He cut off the rising note of emotion in her voice. "Brooke, listen to me. Your brother's not going to disown you for setting off a burglar alarm. And your mother isn't going to fall apart over anything you do. She's been through the worst. She probably knows more about what was really happening than you think she does."

"You're wrong," she blurted. She shook her head, fighting the constriction in her throat that threatened to choke off her voice. "You don't know her. She doesn't know *anything* that's happened. She's never suspected anything I've done or found. And if she ever found out about—"

She stopped herself before she finished the sentence, but she couldn't stop the picture in her mind, of a white envelope stuffed with five thousand dollars in twenties and fifties in the drawer of her father's desk. Panicked, she searched his face. Had he read that thought?

She couldn't tell. But the dark gaze softened with some kind of empathy. His hands moved from her elbows to the back of her arms in a slow, evocative caress.

"Brooke," he said in a gruff murmur. "I know what's between us. You don't know how much I wish—" He broke off, his eyes locked with hers, his hands compelling her inexorably closer. "You don't know how much I want..."

She waited, caught between apprehension and a surge of sharp, forbidden desire, for him to lower his head to hers, close the last few inches between them. His hands on her arms slid higher until his fingertips were tucked between the inside of her arms and the edge of her breasts. Her heart was beating so erratically, she didn't know if what she felt was panic or anticipation.

Conflicting impulses tore at her emotions. She wanted to trust him, to touch him, to give herself up to what her body so achingly needed. Yet how could she want that, when he was a threat to all she valued, to the secret she was trying to protect?

Her voice was a ragged thread, but it carried the desperation of her confused inner struggle. "You could drop the investigation... just leave it alone..." she whispered, her voice heavy with unconscious longing.

She heard him draw in a strident breath. He tipped his head back, away from hers. His eyes slid shut, and she saw a muscle in his jaw tighten until it bulged.

"I can't do that."

"Why not?" It was an agonized plea. "Why can't you?"

Slowly, with rigid control, he pushed her away from him until he was holding her at arm's length.

He drew in a long, shaky breath and held it while he searched her face. The muscle in the side of his jaw worked again. "I can't do that, Brooke," he repeated, with the beginning of anger. "Not even for what you're offering."

For a moment she felt only the anguished protest of frustrated desire. Then the enormity of that brief exchange struck her.

He was an honest, dedicated, single-minded...*cop*. And she had just asked him to do something that he would consider criminal.

"I didn't mean...I never..." She pressed a hand against her stomach. "I wasn't trying to...to bribe you. I didn't mean it that way." She broke off, letting out a rush of breath.

"How did you mean it?" he said, his voice granite-hard.

"I...don't know how I meant it. I wasn't thinking about—"

"About what?" he said accusingly. "Obstruction of justice? Immorality? Police corruption?"

"No!" She wrenched herself away from him and took a step back. Anger surged through her, hot, guilty, irrational. "No, I wasn't thinking of any of those things," she spouted in a sudden display of temper.

"What the hell were you thinking about, then?"

She backed away another step, belligerent and defensive, gesturing angrily. "I was thinking about...my family. About the people who matter to me. And I was thinking about...*us*," she said, flinging out the word defiantly, too upset to care that she was being emotionally reckless. "I wasn't thinking about laws! I was thinking about people, and people will always be more important to me than laws, *Sergeant*. More important than justice or solving cases or your precious, sacred code of honor!"

He stared at her, his face and body a study in rigid emotion, his shoulders stiff with tension, his jaw clenched.

There was a long, charged silence. "I'll get my briefcase and go," Brooke managed to say finally. She backed away another step, then turned away from him.

"Brooke—"

She walked out of the kitchen, her back straight. The bobtailed cat had curled up on the couch, half on top of her briefcase. She yanked it out from under him, and he meowed in protest. "Sorry, Tarzan," she muttered to him. "But the rest of the couch is yours." She drew in a breath. "Just watch your step, cat. And don't ever get yourself on the wrong side of the law."

Marc was standing in the kitchen doorway, watching her. "Why?" he said, his voice as angry as hers. "What do you think I'd do? Cart him off to jail?"

She straightened. "Maybe you would. That's your job, isn't it?"

She turned quickly and crossed the expanse of hardwood to the door before he could answer, her briefcase clutched in front of her like a shield.

Seven

"**H**ey, Brooke! Home run, come on! Give it all you got."

Brooke grimaced at her brother, then turned a sour face toward the pitcher and lifted her bat. The young man on the pitcher's mound was one of her brother's friends. Billy had invited everyone he knew to the annual Shelburne cookout, despite their mother's reluctance to hold the event this year, and despite Brooke's irritation that Billy was pushing it. It had always been Bill Shelburne's party. Her father had been the one to organize the event, issue the invitations, preside over the grill, take care of the check that the losing team contributed to a local charity. But Billy had insisted the three of them could do it, and her mother, to Brooke's surprise, had finally agreed.

"Heads up, Brooke," the pitcher called.

Brooke couldn't remember his name. Like Billy, he was a rookie cop, full of enthusiasm and dedication. She lifted her chin toward him and gripped the bat.

He wound up, threw the softball in what looked like an easy arc, right over the plate—and Brooke's swing missed it. The opposing team chortled approval.

Her own team was pointedly silent, with the exception of Billy. "Come on, Sis. Get with it! We need one of your homers. What happened to your style?"

"It's out in left field," Brooke muttered under her breath.

The pitcher grinned at her, pulled his hat down, and lobbed another pitch.

Brooke gripped the bat, stopping her swing before it started.

"Strike!" Pete Carter yelled.

From behind the stacks of hamburgers on the table beside the grill, her mother glanced toward her, a puzzled frown on her face. Disgusted with herself, Brooke straightened and let the end of the bat fall to the dirt at her feet. She wasn't going to hit a damn thing. She knew it.

"*Brooke,*" her brother agonized, "you're not even watching the ball! Stay over your knees. You're forgetting everything Pop ever told you! Like this!" From the edge of the lawn, he demonstrated batter's posture. The pitcher glanced from him to Brooke, amused.

"Just pitch it, okay?" Brooke snapped.

The pitcher complied. She swung and missed. There was a collective groan from her side of the lawn and an overly dramatic, "Strike Three!" from Pete.

She dropped the bat, jammed her hands into her pockets and turned her back on all of them.

"Never mind, Brooke," one of her brother's friends called, grinning. "You're still good-looking."

Shoulders hunched, Brooke stalked toward the house.

"Brooke?" Billy called after her. "Brooke!"

The door banged shut behind her and she let it, feeling childish irritation underscored by a darker, more adult depression.

She crossed the kitchen floor to the refrigerator, opened the door and stood staring into it. Nothing she saw on the shelves promised ease to her self-critical reflections or the sense of dissatisfaction she'd been living with since she'd last seen Marc Lasaralle.

She sighed and shut the refrigerator door. Every time she thought of what she'd asked him to do, she felt a pang of guilt that stubbornly refused to be reasoned away with the crumbling arguments of a loyalty. She'd meant what she said to him in the heat of anger and frustration. But when her anger had cooled, her conviction had ebbed away like the water in a storm drain after the storm.

She leaned her forehead against the cool surface of the refrigerator.

"Brooke?"

She spun around, startled. "Oh. Billy."

"You okay?"

"Yes, I'm fine," she lied. "I just came in for a cold drink and a couple of aspirin. I'll be out in a minute."

She opened the refrigerator door again and got out a soft drink, then reached into the cabinet for the aspirin, all her movements conveying the brisk message that she was okay, this was just routine, Billy could leave.

When she turned around he was leaning on the counter, watching her through doubt-filled eyes. "Brooke...you haven't been fine for a couple of weeks now. Mom noticed it, too. She's worried about you."

Brooke felt her shoulders slump. She set the soft drink on the counter, unopened. "She doesn't have to be. I've just been a little...preoccupied lately."

Billy met her quick glance, then crossed his arms in front of his chest and stared at the floor, obviously reluctant to drop the subject. "Look, Sis, does this have anything to do with Marc Lasaralle?"

"*What?*"

He glanced away from her.

"Why would you say that?"

"You've been seeing him, haven't you, Sis?"

"No!" She shook her head. "No, I haven't been seeing him! Where did you hear that I had?"

He shrugged, glancing at his feet again. "One of the guys saw you with him at the station the other day. In the...ah...interrogation room. You know, they have that one-way glass...."

Brooke muttered an epithet, shutting her eyes.

"I, ah, think you should know, Sis. I called him. I invited him here today."

The aspirin bottle slipped out of her fingers and clattered on the counter. Brooke snatched it up, turning her back on Billy. Her hand gripped the edge of the sink. "Marc Lasaralle is coming here?" she said in a strained voice.

Behind her, Billy sighed. "No, I don't think he is."

She glanced over her shoulder at him.

"He said he didn't think he could make it."

Brooke let out her breath.

"It took him a real long time to answer, Sis. He *said* he had to work, but Charlie had already told me he wasn't on the roster for today."

"I don't understand what your interest is in this, Billy!"

"Well, I just thought . . ."

"You might have asked me first."

"Yeah," Billy said, with an apologetic shrug. "But I figured it might be sort of a surprise, you know? I . . . guess it backfired."

Brooke didn't answer. She twisted open the cap to the aspirin bottle and shook out two tablets.

"It sounds like you two had a serious fight, or something."

"It's none of your business!" she snapped, then sighed and added, more gently, "Anyway, it's not what you think."

Her brother pushed his hands into his back pockets with an awkward, boyish hesitation. "I know I'm not Pop, Brooke, but if you want someone to talk to, to supply a man's point of view—"

"Billy," she spouted in disbelief, "this isn't about hearts and flowers and romance." She shook her head, half exasperated, half touched by his attempt to fill her father's place for her. "And even if it were, you don't have to be Pop." Her expression softened. "You can just be you, Billy. Just be a brother."

He gave her a trial grin. "Well, maybe I could help as a brother, then. Give you another perspective, an idea what the guy might be thinking, or something."

She turned away from him, staring out the kitchen window. "I don't have any trouble knowing what he thinks," she said defeatedly.

Billy moved toward her, his sneakers squeaking on the linoleum floor, then unexpectedly, she felt his hand, a little tentative and uncertain, on her shoulder. "Hey, I'm sorry, Sis."

She glanced at him, then put her hand over his and squeezed it. "Don't worry about it, Billy. It's . . . nothing to worry Mom about. And anyway—" she found a grin "—aren't you supposed to be up to bat? You'd better get the homer I missed. We're getting creamed out there."

He grinned back at her. "Yeah, well, it ain't over till it's over."

"Go get 'em, slugger." She pulled the tab off the can of soda and offered it to Billy.

He reached for it, took a swallow and handed it back, then turned to go outside. He stopped just before he pushed open the door. "Brooke?"

"What?"

"I hope things work out for you. I think Pop would have liked him—Marc Lasaralle, I mean."

She watched the screen door close behind him while her smile faded and the irony of the statement seeped into her like cold rain through a cotton jacket.

Billy's blind admiration of their father grated on her in a way she'd never been aware of before, and her urge to shake him—to force him to see reality—made her feel guiltier than ever.

She picked up the can of soda and, on impulse, walked through the living room to her father's den. She stood for a moment behind the desk, then ran her fingertips over the back of the old wooden office chair, worn smooth by years of use. Nothing in the office had been changed since he'd last been in it. His keys were in the desk drawer where he'd always kept them. She got them out, unlocked the file cabinet and reached behind the stack of folders in the second drawer. The envelope was still there.

The Lum's News & Tobacco address in the upper left corner was a little smudged and wrinkled, as if it had been handled many times. She slid her finger inside and riffled the edge of the thick stack of bills. Old twenties and fifties. Like the envelope: used, wrinkled, a little dirty.

Maybe more than a little.

She shoved the envelope back behind the files, slammed the drawer shut and pushed the locking button.

Maybe she was wrong. Maybe the purpose of that money had been totally innocent. Maybe she should trust her father's character and let Marc Lasaralle find out the truth. Maybe it wasn't what she was afraid of....

Leaning her aching head against the cool metal of the file cabinet, she let her shoulders slump in dejection.

As if she had any choice in what Marc Lasaralle would do. She couldn't stop him. She couldn't even decide if she had any right to try.

She heard the faint squeak of the kitchen door as someone opened it, then let it slam shut. She straightened, dropped her father's keys into his drawer and walked back through the living room, hardly seeing her surroundings, and let herself out the back door.

The softball game was still in progress. In the batter's place was her mother, clutching the bat awkwardly, aiming a self-conscious grin at the cheering section at the edge of the lawn. The pitcher cocked his hat, wound up and lobbed the softball right over the plate. There was a solid thud as wood made contact with rubber, and Brooke watched in amazement as the ball sailed out over the flower beds into the part of the lawn designated as left field.

"Way to go, Mom!" Billy yelled from the sidelines.

Brooke's mother watched the ball go, her mouth an O of surprise, her expression comically bewildered. She glanced around her, caught sight of Brooke in the doorway, and hesitated.

Brooke gave a wide, surprised grin. "What are you waiting for?" she shouted. "Run!"

She joined in the cheering as her sandal-clad, unathletic mother rounded first base and made it, panting, to second.

The infielder caught up with the ball, snatched it and fumbled.

"Go for it! Run!" Billy yelled as his mother jogged toward third. All the players were on their feet, cheering her on.

From the opposite bench Brooke saw one of the opposing team members cup his hands and shout, "Way to go, Mrs. Shelburne!"

She had passed third and was headed for home before the fumbling outfielder picked up the ball again. "Run, Mom!" Brooke shouted, and her mother put on an extra burst of speed that brought her sliding into home plate seconds before the ball connected with the catcher's mitt.

"Safe!" Pete yelled.

Billy gave an ecstatic war whoop as the field broke into applause. Brooke, grinning from ear to ear, stamped and applauded along with everyone—their team and the opposing team alike. Pete was pounding her mother on the back and laughing delightedly. The pitcher had dropped his mitt to clap louder. Her brother's teammates had linked arms in an impromptu victory dance.

And Marc Lasaralle was standing just behind them, applauding the home run but scowling straight at Brooke.

She froze, her hands poised for clapping, as a heavy lump of dread sank into her stomach and a warning shivered along her nerve endings. *What was he doing here?*

"Hey, Mom, that deserves a beer." Bily wrapped an arm around his mother's shoulders and turned her toward the back steps. "Brooke!" he called. "Get Mom a beer, will you?"

"No, no. A can of ginger ale," her mother protested, flushed and laughing as she and Billy climbed the steps.

Distracted, Brooke tore her eyes away from Marc, but Billy glanced over his shoulder in the direction she'd been looking, and caught sight of Marc. "Hey," he crowed in surprise. "Sergeant Lasaralle. Come on over and get a beer."

His delighted grin swung back to Brooke, then died as it met the expression on her face. She stood where she was, silent in deference to her mother but wishing she could fling the whole party in Billy's face as Marc Lasaralle made his way toward them. He looked as if he hadn't smiled in two days.

Her brother had the grace to sound slightly subdued as Marc stopped on the step in front on them and Billy introduced him. "Mom, Sergeant Marc Lasaralle."

"We're so pleased you could make it, Sergeant," Brooke's mother said. "Billy was afraid you wouldn't be able to join us."

"I'm glad I could," Marc told her, shaking her outstretched hand. "And congratulations on that homer." His dark gaze flicked toward Brooke, and the momentary softening she'd seen in his eyes disappeared. The flash of accusation in that look was almost palpable.

Billy glanced from Marc to Brooke uneasily. Her mother, still smiling, turned toward Brooke. "Perhaps you could get Sergeant Lasaralle something to drink, dear."

"Yeah, Sis. Why don't you get him a beer, and Mom and I'll check the grill."

Damn Billy and his well-meaning interference! She felt color rise in her face as she gave her mother a strained smile.

The pleased, maternal satisfaction faltered a little. "Are you all right, dear?" she murmured.

"Yes, of course. I'm just surprised, Mom. Billy forgot to tell me he'd invited Marc." She forced another smile that faded in the face of Marc's relentless solemnity. Desperate, she tipped her chin up and almost met his eyes. "Can I get you a beer?"

"No, thanks."

The blunt answer and her mother's increasingly worried expression sent a wave of anger coursing through her. "I'll get you a soda, then," she said shortly. She turned her back on him and walked through the kitchen door. If he wanted to stand on the porch with her family, he could do it by himself.

The screen door squeaked open and shut behind her. She ignored it, reaching into the refrigerator for a soda.

"Don't bother," he said to her back. "I don't want anything to drink."

With deliberate movements, she set the can back on the shelf, straightened and closed the refrigerator door, then turned around, aware of the tight muscles in the back of her neck. "What do you want, then?"

"A chance to talk."

She said nothing. Her shoulders ached with tension. She worked her hands into her pockets.

"Billy forgot to tell you he asked me here?" he said after a moment.

"No, he didn't forget." Marc's gaze didn't leave her face, but she found she couldn't hold it. She stared at her feet. "It was the first thing that came to my mind," she muttered. "I didn't know what to say in front of my mother."

"Why didn't you tell her the truth?" he asked. There was a touch of irritation in the tone.

"Because she has enough worries of her own without any added ones from me."

He didn't answer, and the silence felt accusing.

"What do you want me to do?" she burst out defensively, pulling her hands out of her pockets to fling them wide in an angry gesture. "Say things that I know will hurt people just because that satisfies your absolute standards of truth?''

There was a pause, filled with Marc's dark, angry glare. "Did it ever occur to you that life is not a press release?''

She felt her flush deepen. "Is that what you came here to say?''

"No. I came here because your brother invited me. Because I respect the fact that he wants to carry on a good tradition that your father started, and because I was honored that he wanted to include me.''

Her gaze flickered toward him in a quick, surprised acknowledgment of a straightforward honesty she hadn't expected. The sharp reply on the tip of her tongue deserted her. She dropped her eyes, her defensiveness spent.

"I almost didn't come here today," he went on. "I didn't want to see you. Every time I've thought about what happened at my house two days ago, it made me see red. I wanted to take your damn bribe and fling it back in your face.''

She felt herself flinch in a small, unforeseen reaction. "Isn't that what you did?" she said dully.

"Not quite. I just stood there and let you give me some self-righteous line of bull telling me how you care about people, not laws.''

She crossed her arms protectively in front of her, hunching her shoulders. "It . . . wasn't just a line. I do care about people.''

"Well, I care, too," he exploded. "Who the hell do you think you're talking to—the KGB? I care about people, too, while I'm out there enforcing the law. Only I'm a cop, so I'm supposed to care about all of them. I'm supposed to care about the ones who get hurt when those laws are broken. Did you ever consider them? Or the ones who count on somebody having a code of honor?"

She raised her eyes and met his. There was no way she could doubt that he cared. His feelings were in his eyes, his face, his body language. He wasn't trying to hide anything. She was the one with something to hide. Again, her deceptions made her feel petty and small. "I . . . I know that."

"Yeah?"

"Marc . . . it . . . wasn't a bribe."

"It *was* a bribe." His gaze was even, hard, relentless. "No matter how you meant it, no matter what you want to call it, that's what it was. And I've spent the past two days furious at myself because I didn't say that when you were standing in my kitchen." He laughed once, ruefully. "Then I figured out that what I was really furious about was that I was tempted."

Startled, she flicked her gaze toward him for a swift, unguarded moment.

A corner of his mouth quirked up. "Yeah. I was tempted. It seems my absolute standards are a little shaky where you're concerned, Brooke."

His eyes studied her face, then almost involuntarily, swept down over her body. Touched by that look, she felt warmth spread through her. She hugged her arms more tightly, looking back at him. The swift recollection of what had almost happened in his kitchen brought a tiny jolt to her pulse.

"It costs plenty to admit my values aren't as solid as I've always thought." There was a flash of something like vulnerability in his dark eyes, surprising because she didn't expect it. "But shaky or not, they're still in place," he said. "And I wanted you to know it." He let out a breath. "And I guess I needed to say it for myself."

The last of her anger melted away in the face of his total honesty, leaving only a guilty ache of conscience. She let one hand drop to her side. "I...never doubted that, Marc."

He was silent, watching her.

She shrugged, hesitant and uncertain, one hand still holding the opposite elbow. "I didn't go to your house to talk you out of doing what you thought you had to do. It wasn't . . . on my mind at all. I . . . never thought of you as anything but a good cop."

His eyes slid shut for a moment, and she saw the muscle work in his jaw. "Yeah. Maybe that's the trouble." His mouth curved in an ironic smile, and he let out a long breath, looking at her again. "I don't feel like being a cop when I'm around you. I never have. Not from the first time I saw you. I knew I was supposed to think of you as a suspect, but I couldn't do it. I couldn't believe you were guilty of anything. I just wanted to take whatever you said as the gospel truth, without questioning it. I wanted to just...trust you."

She tore her gaze away from his and spun around, unable to face him, feeling utterly unworthy of his trust, yet conscious of how much she needed it. To have him trust her, believe her. She needed it the way she needed his look . . . the sound of his voice . . . his touch . . .

She heard him take a step toward her. She could almost feel the heat of his body along her shoulders, against her back. "Brooke..."

His breath stirred her hair, and she felt a coil of response in her midsection. *No. Don't do this to me, Marc. I can't resist you again.*

He touched her shoulder, and a shiver of sensuality shimmered down her spine. The shuddering breath that went out of her lungs made an involuntary sound in her throat. "Don't...do that," she said, her voice a raveled thread of whisper. "We're not on the same side, Marc. You can't—" Her voice broke, but the rest of the words were a silent cry in her mind: *You can't trust me.*

"Brooke, if there's any way I can keep your father out of this, I will. You have to know that. And...it might have nothing to do with him. His involvement might have been accidental."

He pressed his palm against her shoulder. She wanted to tip her face toward it and caress it with her cheek. But instead she covered her face with her hands and pressed her fingers against her eyes as if she could blot out the picture of that dirty white envelope in her father's file.

"Brooke...sometimes things get turned around. You can't understand them until you know the whole truth. I know what that's like. He was a cop, too."

"Marc...there are things you don't know..." She stopped, the words stuck in her throat. But she'd almost said them. She wanted to say them. She squeezed her eyes tight shut, aware of the ache in her throat, the tension in her stomach. *I'm sorry, Pop. But you didn't raise us to be on the wrong side of the law.*

"Marc...there's..." She couldn't bring herself to say it. Words were too bald, too damning. She couldn't use words. She dropped her hands to the counter, gripped it momentarily, then twisted away from Marc's hand and started toward her father's office.

Marc snatched her hand, then gripped her wrist. "Don't run away, Brooke. Not this time."

The tremor that ran through her as she met the flare of passion in his dark, determined gaze left her too surprised to speak. He moved a step closer. Slowly, slowly his hand brushed up her arm until his fingers cupped the smooth flesh just below her shoulder. His free hand circled her other arm in the same way. His eyes locked with hers and he drew in a shuddering breath, while the pressure of his hands drew her inexorably closer.

Brooke watched his face come nearer, blotting out the light from the back door. For an odd moment she was back in his kitchen, surrounded by the mellow warmth of hand-finished wood, with his grandmother's tomatoes on the windowsill, with the bobtailed cat stalking across the floor, with Marc moving toward her in the wrinkled baseball jersey that clung to his wide, muscled chest the way she wanted to herself, and the words that had divided them so sharply hadn't yet been said.

His mouth came down over hers, slanting against it with sudden, rough urgency, and when her lips opened in response, his tongue slid into the warm, wet confines of her mouth in an intimate, searching claim of possession that set her trembling.

Behind her closed eyelids a spark of light exploded across an inky, velvet blackness and burst into flame with the swiftness of wildfire. She felt the heat and hunger of that fire in her stomach, her legs, her hips, in Marc's hands on her upper arms, his mouth pressed against hers. Hunger shivered through her as thoughts of her divided loyalties, her gnawing conflict, the envelope in her father's files, all vanished into smoke, as if they were consumed by the fire that his touch had started.

His hands moved from her upper arms to grip her shoulders, palms spread wide, but his mouth never left hers and his tongue never stopped its sensuous, sinuous invasion.

She rested her fingers on the waistband of his chinos, her fingers just brushing the strong muscles beneath his shirt.

He made a sound deep in his throat, and all of Brooke's senses responded with a burning passion. Her arms tightened around him, pulling him closer. He groaned again, and Brooke felt the refrigerator door against her back and her neck as Marc's hard chest pressed against her breasts, his hips thrust against her stomach, his thighs molded the top of her legs, and the pressure of his hands, warm in contrast to the cool refrigerator, brought her ever closer, as if he were trying to make their bodies one entity, one flame of passion.

Her heart was thudding, and she strained against him, hungry for his heat, his taste, his fire.

He tore his mouth away from hers and wrenched his hands from beneath her shoulders to thread his fingers into her hair. "Brooke..." The word was a rasping groan. "Don't disappear this time. Don't leave me wanting you."

Her own voice was breathless, the words cut off as his mouth claimed her again. "I'm not . . . going—"

His hips thrust again, rocking her against the hard, heated apex of his thighs, and a tremor shuddered through her at the awareness that he was fully aroused, ready for her, willing her to know the extent of his need.

When he lifted his head again, his eyes stayed shut and he drew in a shaky breath. His hands skimmed down her arms and cupped her buttocks, kneading the rounded muscle through the stiff denim of her jeans, then clasping and pressing her against his hips.

Over his shoulder, Brooke was dimly aware that the light from the screen door shifted, then she heard the squeak of the spring being stretched open. There was a startled, incoherent mutter of surprise that turned into a tuneless whistle sliding up and then down the scale. The door banged shut, and her brother's white-clad back moved away down the porch steps.

Marc turned his head toward the sound and let out a long breath that sent shivers of pleasure through her. He didn't release her, and she felt his chest rise and fall as he drew in a lungful of control.

"Brooke, what do you do to me? You make me forget where I am, what I'm doing. You make me forget everything but this." His hands tightened on her backside.

His words, his hands, the heat of his passion made her knees weak.

"Let me make love to you, Brooke. Let me love you."

She clung to him, trembling, her breath as broken as his. "Not . . . here," she murmured hoarsely

He dipped his head to bring his mouth against the side of her neck. "No," he said against her skin. His voice vibrated against the sensitive cord of her neck. "Not here."

He raised his head just far enough so that she could meet his dark gaze, filled with passion, determination, acceptance of something inevitable as rain. Slowly he slid his hands up her back, then braced them against the refrigerator on either side of her head.

His gaze stayed locked with hers for a span of time filled only with the sound of strident, rushed breath and the quiet hum of the refrigerator. Then he pushed himself upright, wrapping an arm around her shoulders and tucking her against his side as he turned them both toward the living room and walked them out the front door.

Eight

———

Marc's car was parked two houses down the street, behind all the earlier arrivals. He led her down the front steps and around the lilac bushes to cut across the lawn. Through the leaves of the maple that shaded the sidewalk, a breeze rustled, muting the distant sounds of the backyard softball game, cooling Brooke's heated skin where it touched her.

Marc's strong arm around her shoulders kept her close, but he didn't speak except to murmur, "Let's take my car," as they approached it.

"All right." His rib cage just skimmed her side, and his thigh brushed hers as they walked. The touch filled her senses, intoxicating her as if she'd drunk the whole cooler full of beer at the softball game they were walking out on. "Anyway, my car's parked in the driveway. Five people would have to move before we could get out, and then we'd have to explain why we were leaving in the middle of the game."

She felt his head turn toward her. There was a grin in his voice. "Is that okay? For us to sneak out without saying anything to anyone?"

"My brother will cover for us." She glanced up at him with a slightly self-conscious smile. "He thinks you're the best thing to come down the pike since my dad."

"Yeah?" Their steps slowed as they neared his car, and he stopped on the sidewalk, moving her to face him, his arm still around her shoulders. His grin faded to a pensive seriousness. "What about you, Brooke? What do you think?"

She could no more have concealed her honest answer than she could have stopped breathing. "Yes," she said, her voice husky. "I think so, too."

His arm slid from her shoulders, and his fingers trailed into the hair at the nape of her neck for a sweet, short caress before he turned and opened the car door for her.

Her eyes lingered on his strong, sun-darkened hand, the muscles of his forearm, his powerful biceps. She wanted him to touch her again. Excitement rippled through her. She wanted to kiss him, to touch and explore. Her breasts felt full and achingly sensitive. The slight breeze on her bare thighs raised goose bumps of sensuality. She wanted him in her bed, in her body, as close to her as she could hold him. She was eager and ready and already melting in his heat.

She'd been feeling that heat since she'd met him. She'd first denied it and then fought against it, but her resistance had ended. She'd lied to him about all sorts of things from the moment she'd seen him, but her body couldn't lie about the way she wanted him now.

She slid into the car seat and let him shut the door for her, then, in the side-view mirror, watched his legs as he walked around the back bumper. He got into the driver's side.

The sleeve of his blue polo shirt stretched over his biceps as he pushed the key into the ignition. His loose khaki chinos hugged his thighs only enough to suggest the ridges of muscle. She'd seen him in chinos and polo shirt before, and had forced herself not to imagine what he looked like without them. Now the thought that he would pull the shirt up over his head, unbutton and unzip the pants, made her breath catch.

He glanced toward her. "My house?"

"No, mine," she said, the word hoarse. "It's closer."

He nodded, and his mouth curved in a swift, slight smile. She watched it, fascinated. His mouth looked kissed. The wide, masculine contour of his lips was softened, more sensual, by the evidence of her claim on him. She let out a quick breath and raised her eyes to his. He was looking at her breasts. Beneath the stiff, unrevealing cloth of the rugby shirt, she could feel her nipples harden.

Marc's hand tightened on the steering wheel. He backed up the car and pulled out into the shady street.

It was a short drive to Brooke's street, and Marc negotiated it with a policeman's sense of direction and knowledge of the city. Brooke watched him, quiet.

Just past Trinity College the police radio crackled and the dispatcher's voice rasped out in a static burst.

Brook jumped, startled out of her reverie, and Marc glanced toward her.

She met his eyes, then looked away quickly, beset by sudden, niggling doubts. He was a cop. She'd spent the better part of the past two weeks avoiding him. What was she doing now?

He leaned across the dashboard and snapped off the radio. In the renewed silence, he looked at her again.

Brooke turned her head to study the passing line of houses. There was a twinge of panic in her stomach. Maybe what she was doing was all wrong. They weren't allies. She hadn't yet told him about the envelope in her father's files...about the money. Maybe it wasn't too late to back out, to stop this....

"Brooke?"

She almost didn't look at him.

"I won't tell you not to think about your father. I know you can't just shut that off on demand. But think of me, too, okay? As something besides just a cop."

"Are you reading my mind again?"

It was said with a smile, but he sensed the strain behind the lightly spoken words.

"No. It doesn't work that way. I can't read minds. All I can do is guess what you're thinking, and hope you're not having doubts, and worry about what I'm going to do if you change your mind and leave me out in the cold."

"In the cold?"

Her slight smile was welcome reassurance.

"If you leave me outside your door, Brooke Shelburne, I guarantee I'll be cold."

"A strange reaction. Have you had it before?"

"No. I don't react to anyone else the way I react to you."

Her smile lingered, but her eyes shifted away from him uncertainly. "I don't know quite how to take that. I mean—"

"You can take it to mean you've been in my thoughts all the time, Brooke. Waking, sleeping..." He ran a hand through his hair, then glanced at her again. "There've been other women. But there's always been some part of my mind that wasn't there with them. It's not like that with you."

Her eyes were wide, watching him. "No."

"No, what?"

"No, I won't leave you out in the cold." The smile was back, warming him, stoking the eager heat that rose in his chest when he looked at her.

"Come closer, then," he ordered gruffly. He wrapped an arm around her, wondering what reminders of him were there for her.

For him, the reminders were everywhere and not unwanted.

Her street, when they turned onto it, was quiet in the lazy afternoon heat. The trees along the sidewalk barely stirred in the sun-heated air. Marc parked in front of her house, glancing at her before he took his arm from her shoulders to shut off the ignition, thinking of the first time he'd driven her home after he'd apprehended her outside the news store and searched her.

Remembering, he put his arm around her again and ran his palm down the side of her rib cage, lingering at the curve of her waist.

She turned her head toward him. "Are we going to get out?"

"Yes," he said. Her mouth was inches from his— soft, inviting, irresistible. But she moved away from him before he could kiss her, sliding toward the passenger side door and letting herself out.

He got out on the sidewalk and waited for her, then let her precede him along the narrow walkway that led to the outside stairs. The first time he'd taken her home, she'd left him on the sidewalk.

He followed her up the steps, watching her snug white cotton shorts as she climbed the stairs. At the top of those stairs and through the living room was the feminine Victorian bedroom he'd only glimpsed, but that was long enough to have it engraved in his mind.

There was a new, antitheft lock on the door. Marc glanced at it but said nothing, sensing her nervousness as she fumbled with the new key. He stroked a hand down her back, and she jumped, then gave him a nervous, stiff smile over her shoulder.

The lock clicked open and they went in. The living room felt cool and private, with the curtains, drawn against the sunlight, casting pale green squares of filtered light on the pastel rugs and the hardwood floors. From the bedroom, an air conditioner hummed.

She stopped in the middle of the living room, hesitant, and turned around to face him. It took a moment for her to meet his eyes. "Would you...like a drink?" she asked. Her voice had a breathless, half-desperate quality.

"No, I don't want a drink."

"I just thought..." She trailed off, shut her eyes for a second, then started again. "I'm nervous. What do you do when you bring a man to your apartment in the middle of the afternoon to..."

"You take him into your bedroom."

A ghost of a smile appeared on her face. "You do?"

"Yes. Unless you want him to make love to you on the living-room rug."

"I don't know." She laughed—a high-pitched, tremulous sound. "Do you like rugs?"

"We came this far. We might as well make it to the bedroom."

"Yes. I suppose."

Still she made no move. Marc held out his hand to her. When she took it, he tugged gently to draw her closer, then led her across the living room and the tiny hallway and pushed open her bedroom door.

Cool air, faintly scented and woodsy, surrounded them. Potted plants stood on a white wooden bench by the French doors. The air was scented with herbal fragrances. An ivory, hand-tatted spread covered the four-poster bed.

Marc tightened his grip on Brooke's hand. She pulled it out and wrapped her hands around her elbows in the gesture he recognized as self-protective.

She had to protect herself against him? He gazed at her, drawing in a deep breath, recognizing his own nervousness—and his own need. He needed all of her—her trust, her unashamed hunger, her thoughts, her fantasies, her willingness to share every part of herself. Nothing less would salve the aching, soul-consuming need that had been building within him since the day he'd first seen her. Nothing rushed or forced would be enough. He had to go slowly. He had to have her with him, willing, trusting....

He filled his lungs again with cool air. "It smells good in here," he said softly. "Like...someplace I've been before, but I can't remember where."

"It's the rose geraniums. And the tansy."

The rough velvet of her voice stroked his nerve endings. "Tansy?"

She walked by him to the window bench, plucked a delicate, fernlike leaf from one of the plants and crushed it in her fingers, then held it out toward him. Her face was in shadow, her hair haloed by the leaf-filtered light behind her as she stood perfectly still for a moment, and the clean, aromatic smell of the leaf drifted toward him.

She could have been a wood sprite, inviting him to mysterious pleasures that were half enchantment, half sensuality. She could have been an ancient goddess, at home in the forest she ruled, dark hair spilling over her shoulders like midnight rain, her hands offering some magical talisman.

Marc slowly took three steps toward her and took the leaf from her hand, crushing it in his fingers the way she had. The herbal perfume was sharp, intoxicating, and it tugged at some elusive, sensual remembrance.

He brought his hands together, rubbing the crushed greenery into his palms, then carefully he threaded his fingers into the hair at her temples and ran his hands through her long, dark hair.

She made a soft, startled sound.

"I want you to smell like this, Brooke," he murmured. "I want to smell tansy in your hair. It's beautiful and it suits you."

A slight smile curved her mouth. Her eyes slid shut, and her head tipped back as he ran his hands once again through the black silk of her hair.

A piece of torn leaf fell onto her shirt. Marc picked it up, crushed it once more in his palms, then spread his fingers and trailed his fingertips along the sides of her neck to stroke the hair at her nape. Brooke shivered when he lifted the hair from her shoulders.

"Are you cold?"

She shivered again even while she murmured, "No." The cool draft from the air conditioner touched the back of her neck, but his hands were so warm, so sensuous....

Brooke lightly rested her hand on the back of Marc's elbows as he circled her neck and slipped his fingers inside the collar of her shirt. His strong fingers explored the top of her spine, then his hands caressed the hollows where her shoulders met her neck.

She leaned toward him, eager for more. He stroked the sensitive cords below her jaw with slow, up and down movements of his palms as he, too, leaned toward her and tipped his head down, bringing their mouths closer. He cupped her jaw with his hands as his lips touched hers, lightly, with gentle, unhurried pressure. Her lips parted at the first subtle coaxing, and her tongue sought his in a tentative, first assertion of her desires.

At her response, Marc's hands tightened momentarily on the back of her scalp, then let go to trace her shoulders and her upper arms, down to her wrists. He guided them around his neck and held them there while he opened his mouth wider over hers. Exploring the contours of her mouth, he let her tongue slide along his teeth until his own tongue met hers, caressed, learned, led and followed in a slow, symbolic mating of thcir mouths.

Brooke felt his hands touch her shoulders again, then slide into the hollows beneath her arms, at the top of her rib cage. Slowly, gently, he skimmed his hands down her sides to her waist, then followed the curve of her hip to the hem of her shorts and lower, until his warm, seeking hands rested on her bare thigh. He broke off the kiss and drew in a sharp gasp of air.

"Brooke..."

She murmured something incoherent, focused now on his hands as they retraced their sensuous path along the sides of her body.

"The first time I met you...the first time I touched you, I wanted you like this. Warm...willing..."

She smiled. "And unarmed?"

His exhaled breath stirred the hair at the top of her forehead, and she felt his smile. "Unarmed," he agreed. "You don't need weapons, woman. You made me feel like a...rapist, that day. I was ready to shoot myself. And, God, I wanted you. That's the worst thing a cop can do, but you made me want to break every police rule they ever drummed into us. I was afraid to get too close to you, but I couldn't just let you walk away, Brooke. Charlie was ready to kick my butt across the street, and I knew the Chief would do it for him when we got back, but I couldn't just let you go."

The confession touched her in a way that made her feel as vulnerable as he was willing to be himself. There was a trembling in her stomach that needed the stroking of Marc's hands to calm it. She kneaded the back of his neck, pulling him closer. "I'm not going any-where, Marc."

His lips met hers again and teased them with light, fleeting contact and nibbles at the edge of her mouth. His hands drifted down her sides to her hips, then slipped inside her shirt and brushed up her sides, over the band of her bra, the heel of his hand just brush-ing the lacy cups. The shirt slid from her body as he drew it up over her arms and pulled it over her head. He dropped it behind her.

The bra she wore beneath the unisex, no-nonsense rugby shirt was lacy, feminine, a semitransparent wisp of ivory, and Marc's gaze lingered for a moment, ad-miring, studying, before his hands came back to her sides, his palms just cupping the lower swells of her breasts. His thumb traced an edge of lace from the silk strap to the place where it dipped under her arm, then he caressed her breasts, not touching the nipples, though within the gossamer fabric they were pointed and taut, gathered into rigid knots of desire. Brooke's breath caught in her throat.

"Lace..." Marc said gruffly. His fingertips trailed up the deep, warm valley between her breasts, then moved to the outer curves of her breasts, shaping and caressing, coming closer to their crested peaks, but still not touching. Brooke's hands clasped his shoulders, her grip tightening as she waited.

When finally his thumbs brushed over her nipples and the heat of his palms covered her breasts, she felt a wave of velvet fire that drew a sound from deep in her throat.

"Ah...Brooke...I knew you would feel this way. I knew what sounds you'd make. I knew how beautiful you'd be."

He brushed his knuckles against the distended peaks that strained against the lace of her bra, drawing more husky sounds from her throat as he caressed her with rhythmic, up and down movements.

The sweet agony he roused was half pleasure, half torment, for she needed more of him—skin against skin, heat against heat. She skimmed her hands down his torso, then tugged his shirt, pulling it out of the waistband of his chinos, she slipped her hands underneath it and felt the warm, honed, muscular flesh just above his waist. He pulled the shirt up over his head, then while he stood before her, the shirt still clutched in one hand, his eyes dark with passion, she spread her palms on his chest. With a long sigh of quivering expectation, she explored the hard, almost square pectorals, taut, flat stomach, dark, springy hair across the broadest part of his chest, which trailed down to a point that led into the waistband of his pants. The heat of his skin, the texture of dark hair over hard muscles, the shudder of his response were intoxicatingly new, and yet, somehow, familiar, intimately known, and the foreknowledge was as natural and inevitable as the fire that flared everywhere they touched.

His hands circled her back, and he pulled her against him and claimed her mouth once more in a kiss that was demanding, ardent and abandoned, a tangle of tongues and teeth and the sensitive recesses of their mouths. She arched her back to press her breasts against his chest. Brooke strained in a deep yearning for closeness that seemingly couldn't be satisfied. She moved her body, letting her thighs part so that the most sensitive part of her body rode his thigh, and Marc's hard, hot arousal was pressed against the bony curve of her hip.

He gave a moan of agonized pleasure and tore his mouth from hers. "Ah...Brooke. I want you too much. I'm going too fast for you. And I want you with me." His lips slid along her jaw and trailed hot, silken kisses down the side of her neck to her shoulder. "I need all of you...." he murmured against her skin.

The hot, sensual path of his mouth followed the length of her collarbone to the center of her chest, then moved lower, to the hollow of her breasts, only half covered by the lacy, décolleté bra. She clung to his shoulders as his hands kneaded the sides of her rib cage, and he ran his tongue over the lace-covered peak of her breast. Brooke's knees went weak as with lips and tongue and wet, velvet heat, he shaped and stroked and suckled.

Her shivering response rose to her throat and became a soft moan of aching need. He moved to her other breast to arouse and torment, while his hands tugged the bra straps lower until the lace cup peeled down from her breast, and he drew her hard, sensitized nipple into his mouth.

Brooke's head fell forward, and her fingers uncurled from his shoulder as, lost in sensuality, she let the waves of pleasure wash through her. He pleasured her as if he knew her body as well as his own, his hands and mouth knowing her wants before she arched to meet him, before she moved to offer the other breast, before she sucked in her stomach so that his hand could slip inside the waistband of her shorts.

His warm, wet tongue traced a line from between her breasts to the snap of her shorts, then dipped into her navel as his thumbs unfastened the snap. There was the rasp of a zipper, then she felt Marc's warm palms at her waist, smoothing shorts and panties down over her hips until they dropped to her feet.

His hands shaped her buttocks, her hips, the back of her legs. The knuckles of one hand grazed her inner thigh, sliding up from the knee until he could go no higher, then back down again, in a slow, sensuous, repetitive stroking that made her quiver with desire and brought flutters of sensation to the deep core of her femininity.

"Let me touch you, Brooke," he breathed. The words were a moist caress against her taut stomach.

Her broken murmur of assent was incoherent, but the words weren't needed. She stepped out of the pool of clothes, and Marc's hand slipped up her leg to the sensitive flesh at the apex of her thighs. His gliding touch stroked and explored with consummate care. When his fingers dipped into the hot, secret recesses of her femininity, she felt a rain of pleasure that flooded her senses with readiness and yearning. The abandoned, primitive cry that came from her was like no sound she had ever made; her response to Marc's intimate caresses like none she had ever felt.

His tongue dipped into her navel again, then he kissed the flat expanse of her stomach, moving down, nuzzling the triangle of dark hair at the meeting of her thighs. She drew in a breath and tensed, sensing his destination. Her hands, still constrained by the straps, moved to his head to stop him. "Marc . . . I don't . . . I haven't . . ."

His hands caught her wrists and swept them back
behind her, holding her in a gentle grasp while his
tongue touched her intimately. Her breathless pro-
tests trailed off into a long, shuddering sigh, and her
knees went weak as flames of desire leaped up from
the core of her being and raced along her veins. The
hot, wet velvet of his tongue and lips was a sweet assault that ravished her and brought heat licking along
all the surfaces of her skin. Her knees buckled against
his chest, and her fists closed on the cool, feathery
leaves of the plant that was within her touch. The
smell of tansy drifted up around them, exotic and
heady, firing senses already transported to some sensual, separate space and time.

He straightened, standing in front of her and sup-
porting her with one arm while he tipped his mouth to
hers, and as if in response to her unvoiced, ardent demand, unfastened the button of his pants with his free
hand and let them drop around his ankles. He stepped
out of them and kicked them aside, then reached behind Brooke to unclasp, one-handed, the hook of the
bra that hung around her waist. The lace fell to the
floor.

Brooke raised her fists, still grasping the tansy
leaves, to his hard, broad chest. Slowly she opened her
fingers and flattened her palms against his skin. The
pressure she brought against his muscled chest was
minimal, but Marc responded to it as if she were all-
powerful and not to be resisted. He took two steps
back until he came up against the edge of the bed. He
sank down onto it, reaching for her to pull her with
him as he lay back against the ivory bedspread.

Leaning over him, her knees braced on either side of his, Brooke ran her hands down his chest, leaving a trail of crushed leaves and pungent, herbal scent. She stroked his rib cage, his flat, ridged stomach, the pattern of sleek dark hair that arrowed down to his groin. He lay still under her hands, only his labored breath and the heat of his body betraying his effort at control. When she lifted her hands and touched him with her fingertips for the first time, his hips jerked once. Then his hands covered hers, guiding her warm palms closed around him while he let out a long, hoarse breath. She stroked and explored, reveling in her power to arouse him, in the deep, feminine urge to know his body, that urge adding to her own trembling sensuality. Marc's hands moved over her as she straddled him, each touch, each stroke, each intimate caress bringing them both closer to the inevitable, ultimate intimacy of shared pleasure and power.

"Yes . . . yes, like that . . ." Marc groaned, and then his hand moved to stop her and a strangled sound cut off his voice for an instant. "But not again, Brooke. Not so soon. I want you with me." Her eyes, closed in the all-encompassing experience of sensation, opened and met his, and his dark gaze held her as if by some hypnotic intensity. "I want you with me, Brooke," he rasped again. "I want your fire."

"Yes," she whispered. "Yes . . . now . . ."

She moved her hips higher on his body, instinctively seeking to assuage the aching hunger of her body.

There was no longer any question of lengthening the inevitable, unstoppable prelude to their joining. "Yes. Now," Marc groaned in answer to her. He grasped her hips and guided himself into her with one slow, powerful thrust.

Brooke clutched his shoulders and her eyes slid shut, blocking out the dappled sunlight, the lace-covered bed, the familiar bedroom. There was nothing but darkness, the heady scent of herbs, and the exquisite joining of man to woman—and the vision of the fire that ringed them, flickering on dark earth, on the tall, angular oaks that seemed to tower over them, stirred by restless wind and shadowed by deep darkness.

Marc let himself feel the earth, the wind, the heat of the fire. Each slow thrust and retreat of his hips was echoed in the sounds of heightened ecstasy that were drawn from Brooke's throat and escaped into the dark oak forest beyond the circle of fire. He heard his own voice, a low counterpoint to the womanly sounds of passion stoking his own heated rush to completion. The crush of velvet-leaved plants and dark, fertile earth beneath them cradled their straining bodies as if it gave back, measure for measure, the sweet torment of unbearable tension that moved them closer...closer...

There was something else—some smoky mist that moved at the edge of the forest, but he couldn't see beyond the ring of fire that enclosed them, couldn't sense anything beyond the sleek heat of the woman whose body enclosed his, couldn't feel anything beyond the striving of their bodies for release, the yearning of his soul for entwinement with hers, for the oneness that they approached with every beat, every thrust. The power of that striving was like nothing he had known: forceful, all-encompassing, inevitable, almost terrifying in its intensity. Her hands clenched again, and she cried out, and he knew that she, too, felt that moment of terrifying sensation. Then he felt the heat of her body expand suddenly in a release of sexual power that shuddered through her and sent him reeling over the edge of rapture, ecstasy pouring through him and out of him. Fire leaped up around them, burning into an explosion of heat and light, of elements rushing together in the consummation, the joining of the circle of earth, fire, and air.

Trembling, he rolled to his side and held her to him, his mouth seeking hers in the seal that acknowledged their joining. Warm, dark earth, soft beneath their bodies, gave back the heat they had expended, and slowly the fires dimmed and burned down, quieting into the rustling of wind in the oaks above them, murmuring of completion.

Marc let his eyes drift closed. The tangled silk of Brooke's hair, scented faintly with tansy, spilled across his chest. Her hand rested on his side, limp, and her legs were tangled with his. It was where she belonged. It was where they both belonged.

Nine

———

Cool air drifted over Brooke's shoulders and back and chilled her. Still half asleep, she turned on her side, seeking the warmth of Marc's body, finding only empty space and cool sheets. The air conditioner droned in the background, familiar and recognized, but the clink of silver against china, the sense of an unusual presence in her apartment, brought her to full consciousness. She opened her eyes.

Framed by a square of light, Marc stood leaning against the bedroom doorjamb, naked, a cup and a spoon in his hands, his face serious.

"You awake, Ms. Shelburne?"

He must have thrown the bedspread over her when he got up. She pulled it higher on her shoulders as her eyes roved over him—muscular legs, lean hips, the dark patch of hair at the apex of his thighs that did not conceal his unashamed masculinity, the coffee cup clutched in front of his broad, muscled chest. "Why didn't you wake me up?" She passed the back of one hand over her eyes. "What time is it?"

"Nine-thirty."

Her eyes skimmed the darkened room. "So late?" She smiled in apology. "What have you been doing all this time?"

"Prowling around your apartment." He grinned briefly. "Looking for something to eat." His eyes darkened, and the corners of his mouth drifted down into a pensive expression. "Watching you."

Bracing herself on one elbow, she watched him back. She didn't want him standing in her doorway. She wanted him beside her in her bed, the length of his body pressed to hers, warming her, holding her, making her feel feminine and powerful.

He leaned over to put the cup down on the floor, then straightened, his gaze on her. "And I've been thinking, Brooke."

She was caught by his seriousness. Rolling onto her back and covering her eyes with one wrist, she felt reluctant to ask the conventional, *About what?* But she heard her own voice forming the words even as a warning vibrated in her chest. "About what?"

The silence told her how still he had gone. "About who broke into this apartment. About who burned down Lum's and what the connection is."

She squeezed her eyes shut and swallowed.

"About us," he said, while the air conditioner droned on. She felt a chill over her arm, along her side, into the middle of her chest.

"About what we're doing," he said.

She made herself turn her head and look at him. He hadn't said, *About what we did*. She could take some reassurance from that, couldn't she? Watching him, she became wary, a little apprehensive.

He took the two steps toward the bed, leaned down to jerk up a corner of the bedspread, and got under it with her. He turned her toward him, holding her upper arms, and she reached around his waist and pulled him close. A sigh of completeness went through her. She drank in the heat of his body, as if it were sunlight in the darkness. "I don't want to think," she murmured against his skin. "Not...not yet." She closed her eyes. "Maybe not...ever," she whispered, almost too softly for Marc to hear.

He braced himself up on one elbow and slowly stroked her dark hair back from her cheek. Through her closed lids she sensed he was studying her. "It's something we have to think about, Brooke. It has consequences."

"Can't we just...let it be? Just see what happens?"

There was a silence where she knew he was waiting for her to look at him. Reluctantly she opened her eyes.

"No," he said evenly.

"Marc—"

"I'm a cop, Brooke," he said gently. "And I'm involved with a woman who's part of the case I took on. Do you know how many rules that breaks? Do you know how far that strays from the code of ethics I swore to?"

"No." She shook her head. The fingers combing through her hair stopped. "No, I don't know what's so wrong about it." His hand fell to her shoulder and he let out a breath. His eyes, meeting hers, were troubled.

"I'm not asking you to drop the case," she blurted out. "I told you that. You can do whatever you think you have to. I won't ask you to change any of that. What's wrong about it?"

"Because what I have to do is find out the truth, Brooke. Without letting myself develop blind spots. What I have to do is use logic and reasoning and not let my feelings get in the way of that. There are good reasons for all the rules that dictate that a cop can't get involved with a—" his eyes dropped, then he drew in a sharp breath and looked at her again "—with a suspect." His hand cupped her cheek swiftly when she would have turned away. "No matter how willing he is to stake his life on the fact that she's innocent." His voice gentled. "And I would, Brooke. I would. But I haven't got any way yet to convince the Chief of that."

"Charlie said I wasn't suspected of anything!"

"You're not," he cut in. "Nobody believes you set that fire. But the facts of the case say you might be a link to something, or someone." His mouth twisted suddenly with the emotion he was feeling, and Brooke felt an answering response in her own heart, and a pang of guilt, sharp and ragged-edged, lanced through her. He cradled her face in both hands, his long fingers twining into the hair at the nape of her neck. "Damn it, Brooke, someone broke into this apartment. I won't know if you're safe until this is over. You could get hurt. The Chief's going to tell me that. He's going to tell me I could get hurt. Cops get hurt when one of them gets involved with a woman who's off limits.''

She held his wrist, her grip tightening suddenly with the thought of Marc being hurt. And if it were her fault, she'd never be able to bear it. *Tell him,* a voice in her head urged. *Tell him about the envelope.*

"Marc..."

His hands tightened in her hair, and he pulled her face against his shoulder. ''But I am involved, Brooke. And God help me, I couldn't stop myself from wanting you. You've been in my dreams—that place with the fire and the wind in the trees, and you.'' He shifted her onto her back and braced himself over her, while his hair-roughened thigh nudged her legs apart and pressed against the sensitive juncture at the center of her body. When he spoke again, his jaw moved against her cheek and his breath was warm and moist in her ear.

''I knew you were there with me, Brooke, when we made love. I knew it was that way for you, too.''

''Yes.''

''Does that scare you? That...strangeness? Is that something you don't want?''

''No, it doesn't scare me. Not as long as you're with me. And I do... *want*, Marc. As much as it's possible to. As much as you could possibly imagine.''

''I don't have to imagine,'' he said gruffly. He caressed her with his chest, grazing the tips of her breasts with the fine hair that curled over his pectoral muscles. ''I know. And I want it again—surrounded by your fire, listening to the sounds of your forest. I don't want you to be afraid. Not there. Not of me.''

"That's not what I was afraid of," she whispered half to herself. "I never thought it would be like that."

"What did you think it would be like?"

Her hands ceased their slow exploration of his spine for a moment. "That you'd be able to...read my mind. To know all my thoughts."

His lips nuzzled below her ear, then kissed a line along the soft underside of her jaw. "I want to know all your thoughts," he murmured. "I want you to tell them to me." His cheek, just beginning to be roughened by a shadow of beard, scraped gently against the hollow of her throat, when the warm satin of his mouth smoothed away the roughness. "I want to know what you're thinking when I do this...." He kissed the valley between her breasts, then nuzzled the softness by his left cheek, circling the fullest part of her breast. "And this..." He breathed gently on her hardening nipple, then took it into his mouth.

She stopped thinking. The sound that came from her throat told of desire, not logic, and it kept the consequences of their act at bay for a while longer. She welcomed the flood of yearning with the way she arched to meet Marc's mouth and drew her hands down his back. Marc's hands cupped her shoulders. She wanted him again, now, and the tension in his arms that betrayed the extent of his own quick arousal added to her urgent longings, but his mouth at her breasts was slow, unhurried, leisurely. The tender assault devastated her senses and drew soft, longing cries from her throat.

The ring of the phone barely registered in her consciousness at first, so completely had she willed the outside world away, but the ringing persisted, intruded on her senses. Finally, she let out a long sigh, turning toward the doorway through which the sound came. Marc lifted his head. His thumbs caressed her shoulder bones. "Do you need to answer it?" he murmured.

She shook her head. "I have a machine. I can hear the message." Still she resented the intrusion, having to wait out another ring, the click of the tape whirring on.

Her mother's voice, muffled and distant, said, "Brooke? This is Mom." There was an indrawn, uncertain breath. "Oh, Brooke, I wish you were home. I brought the check into your father's office—the softball game check—and I thought I'd put it in his file cabinet, but I found an envelope, Brooke."

Brooke froze, feeling every muscle in her body tense. She was set to push Marc away, dash out to the living room and quiet the damning message by picking up the receiver. But her mother went on before she could move.

"It says, 'Lum's News & Tobacco' on it." The words came in a quavering rush. "There's money in it. Five thousand dollars, in cash, and your father never kept cash around the house. Never! And I don't know what this is! So, would you please call me, honey, as soon as you get in? Do you know anything about this, Brooke?" A silence followed, humming with the tension of the caller and the two people who listened to it, then the receiver clicked, and the tape machine hissed and shut off.

Marc's hands tightened convulsively, biting into her skin for a moment before he consciously relaxed his fingers. His direct, unevadable gaze searched her face while a muscle in his jaw clenched tight.

"*Do* you know anything about it?" he asked finally, the words velvet soft with iron control.

She couldn't find her voice.

"*Do you?*"

Her hand left his back and curled into a fist; her nails dug into her palms. "Yes," she managed through her closed throat. "But I—"

He pushed himself up, spun around and swung his legs over the edge of the bed, propping his elbows on his knees, his face buried in his hands.

Brooke lifted herself on her elbows and half reached for him, then let her hand drop. She clutched the bedspread and pulled it up around her.

"All right," he said curtly. "What do you know about it?"

"N-nothing more than what my mother said. I found it in my father's file cabinet."

"When?" The word was as sharp and hard as chipped stone.

"Two weeks ago."

He stood up with such a violent release of energy that the bedsprings bounced. Heels thudding in the floor, he paced across the room to the pile of clothes they'd dropped in front of the plant bench. Still with his back to her, he grabbed his pants and yanked them on. The zipper rasped, angry and accusing.

Stricken, Brooke followed his movements while she pulled the lacy bed cover up to her chin and scooted up to a half-sitting position against the headboard, knees raised, shoulders hunched as if to make herself as small as possible. "I was going to tell you, Marc," she started. "Only I—"

"When?" He bent over for the shirt, dragged it over his head, punched his arms into the sleeves in a movement that threatened to tear the seams. "After you brought me home with you? After you made love to me? After you waited to see how much of me you could own?"

She recognized the hurt behind the anger, and pain twisted through her. "No! No, Marc, I *was* going to tell you, I tried just before she called, but..."

"But what?" He was staring at her with accusation, his mouth hard, set and uncompromising, and Brooke's desperate explanation trailed off into silence. He was a cop, bound by a code of honor that saw everything in black and white. What could she say to him?

"But you were waiting to see if I could read your mind? How did you feel when you found out I couldn't? Pleased with yourself? Satisfied with your own PR job?" He laughed ruefully. "Well, I'll say this for you, Brooke. You're good at it."

"That's not fair!"

He bent down to pick up his socks, then stood knotting his fists around them so that the skin around his knuckles was white and bloodless. "No?"

"It's my father, Marc. It's not just me. It's my family—my mother and my brother and my father's partner. You don't understand—"

He cut her off with words that scorched in their intensity, though his voice was controlled. "No, lady, *you've* got it wrong. You're the one who doesn't understand. There's been a serious crime here—at least one serious crime. A building was torched and burned to the ground by someone who probably didn't care who got hurt in the process. And you were withholding evidence. That just possibly makes you an accessory before the fact." He bent over again, snatched up her shirt, and tossed it across the bed toward her. "And it makes me one goddamned blind fool."

The room blurred in front of her. Angrily, she wiped at her eyes with one hand.

"Get dressed," Marc ordered. "We're leaving."

"Why? Where are we going?"

"I'm going to drive you back to your mother's house so you can get your car and I can look at that envelope. And on the way, you're going to answer the questions I haven't thought of yet."

He turned, back stiff, and walked out toward the bathroom.

Brooke swallowed the misery in her throat and pressed the heels of her hands hard against her eyes to keep herself from crying. Why in the name of heaven had her mother, who never went into her father's office, chosen this day to open the file cabinet? *There were consequences,* Marc had said. Well, she'd wanted independence. She'd wanted to make her own decisions. And so she'd searched out the missing logbook, she'd concealed information, and, dear God, she'd made love to a man she was lying to.

Now she had to pay the consequences: Marc's anger, his sense of betrayal, his...contempt. In his eyes, she was on the wrong side of the law. She bit down on her lip and pressed her eyes harder as fresh pain washed through her. Through the closed door of the bathroom, she heard the shower run for thirty seconds, then shut off, as if he were too resentful and angry even to use her water. Brooke glanced toward the door, then afraid he'd come out and find her still huddled on the bed as if she were waiting for him, she made her shivering body move. She dragged on her robe, staring bleakly for a long moment at the herbs on her plant bench, then as the bathroom door opened, she snatched some clothes from her closet.

She didn't speak to him on her way to the bathroom, and the stony silence between them lasted until they were seated in his car and he'd turned on the police radio.

The scratchy voice of the dispatcher squawked out information in a code Brooke didn't recognize. Unlike most of the families of cops she had known, hers hadn't had a police band radio in their house when she was growing up. It had been understood that knowing all the police communications would make her mother worry. Whenever Brooke and her brother had listened in Bill Shelburne's patrol car, there had been a certain thrill of the forbidden and dangerous about it. She squeezed her eyes shut and her fingers tightened on the armrest of the door. Was that why she'd had to know about the money? Some childish impulse to seek out forbidden knowledge? To prove she didn't need to be protected?

She glanced across the seat at Marc, and another wave of pain struck her. Even now she felt as utterly defenseless against the longings he stirred as Millie Shelburne had been against her husband's stronger personality.

"Marc . . ." It was a quiet plea.

His dark gaze swung toward her for a moment, hard, uncompromising and still angry, and the unformed apology died on her lips.

There was a flash of dark fire in his eyes, some brief flame of desire that made her heart beat faster, then he snapped his head around to the front. His mouth was a straight, hard line. "The envelope," he said brusquely. "That's why you went to Lum's to search for the logbook? Because you had found the envelope, and you were trying to figure out why."

She nodded, then when he shot her a questioning glance, said, "yes," her voice a scrape of reluctance.

"How did you know the logbook would be there?"

"I didn't. I just guessed."

He glanced at her again. "Where did you find it?"

"Behind a loose brick in the window."

"A space that might have been a drop-off point for money?"

She met his gaze, startled. "I don't know. I didn't find any money there."

"But that night someone broke into your apartment. They weren't looking for a logbook nobody knew you had. They were looking for money, weren't they?"

"I don't know! I don't know any more than that. I wish to God I'd never gone there! Please…please, do we have to talk about it?"

He didn't answer, and her eyes grew bleak as she took in his silence. *Yes, they had to talk about it. It was his case. And he was a cop.*

She twined her hands together in her lap and made her voice even and emotionless. "What are you going to tell my mother?"

"She's your mother. Why don't you talk to her?"

"And what do you want me to say?"

"Try the truth." The tone was bitter, and Brooke turned her head away sharply.

Marc let out a breath and ran a hand through his hair. "Maybe she deserves to know the truth, Brooke. Maybe she wants it. Maybe she's damn sick of having you protect her from something she has a right to know."

The quick anger she felt was welcome. "What do you know about it? What do you know about my family?"

The light at the intersection changed, and Marc slowed for it, deliberately bringing the car to a stop before he turned his dark gaze on her. "I know what it feels like to be lied to."

She stared back at him, unable for a long, tension-filled moment to look away from the gaze in which she read anger, pain and a sense of betrayal that gave her a sharp, unbearable surge of guilt. She had made a choice, and in the process she had hurt and angered a man she trusted, admired, maybe was even in love with. And now she had to face the consequences of her choice. And, dear God, she didn't know if she could do it.

The radio crackled, announced a code fourteen-fifty happening in a familiar downtown block, then repeated the message.

Marc's gaze shot to the radio, and he muttered a clipped, savage curse. His hands tensed on the steering wheel. He swore again, then stomped on the gas, pulling through the light without waiting for it to change.

Brooke's arm shot out as she braced herself against the dashboard. "What is it? Marc?"

"Fire. Someone's been hurt."

Her eyes flew toward the road as if she could see flames. "Where?"

He gave her a swift, unreadable glance. "I'm not sure what the number is." His mouth tightened. "But I know the damn street."

He made a hard right onto a side street. Brooke stared ahead. She knew this area. She'd worked here until three months ago. She saw the flashing lights two blocks before they reached the police barricade. Blue and red. Police and Fire. She could just barely hear the crackle of loudspeakers, but even at this distance, she could smell the acrid, roiling smoke. From the other direction, a siren wailed, then stopped.

Brooke leaned toward the windshield, trying to see. A block later she saw the flames, garish and obscene, roaring up in the midst of the frantic efforts of fire-fighters with hoses. Police vehicles were parked in the middle of the street, cordoning off an area that was made barely recognizable by the urgent determination of an emergency squadron in action.

Her pulse was racing as Marc pulled over to the curb behind the line of cars gathered at the roadblock, and wrenched open the door.

She threw herself out of the car and ran blindly after him, toward the fire, stumbling once at the wrenching shock of realizing that the burning building was Senator Albert Andrew's campaign headquarters.

Smoke and ashes blurred the scene in front of her, and the dull roar of fire masked the shouts of the men fighting it. A couple of hoses had been trained on the structure, and a ladder truck was being backed up to the building. Across the street, an ambulance was parked. A uniformed medic was closing the back door.

"Marc!" A policeman she didn't recognize was sprinting toward them.

Marc halted for a moment, facing him. "Who's been hurt?"

The young cop drew in a ragged breath. "Charlie."

At Brooke's gasp, he glanced toward her, then looked back at Marc.

"He was in front of the building when it blew. He had the window open. He's conscious, but he's got some nasty burns on his arm and his face. I don't know how bad."

"Oh, dear God," Brooke murmured.

Marc looked up to follow the movement of the ambulance just pulling away from the curb. The reddish light played over the clenched muscle in his jaw.

In the smoke and the ashes, her eyes were burning. She felt the pressure of tears and blinked them back, but she could do nothing about the shudder of reaction that racked her body.

"But why was he here?" It was a cry of protest, spoken from the heart, a desperate longing to deny the reality of Charlie's being hurt.

Marc's grim face turned toward her. "He was keeping an eye on the place. We've both been doing that—taking turns."

She swallowed, absorbing the information. The taste of smoke and cinder burned her throat. "And there was an . . . an explosion?"

"Yes. Someone set it off."

"Are . . . are you sure?"

There was a splintering roar as the crane on the ladder truck broke through the roof of the building. Brooke flinched, her gaze on the fire, and Marc's strong hands closed around her shoulders, to support her—or to control her, she didn't know which. He turned her toward his car and walked her back. "We're going to the hospital," he said brusquely.

At his car, he opened the passenger door and put her in, then slammed it shut and jogged around the front to get in on his side. The radio snapped again, with a request for assistance on a seven-twenty-eight. She didn't know what it meant. She didn't know what anything meant anymore.

Ten

The hospital corridor outside Charlie's room was bright, sterile, with trained workers going about their business. Brooke sat, tense and motionless, on a cushioned chair against the wall. The doctor had specified only one visitor at a time, and Charlie's wife had been with him for the twenty minutes since he'd been brought down from Emergency. Across the corridor, as far from her as he could get, Marc leaned against the wall on one raised arm, his back to her. She drew in a breath that seemed to hurt as it expanded the tight ache in her chest. Maybe if she got up, walked across the floor, put her hand on his shoulder...

She bit her lip and clenched her hands around the cardboard cup that held the dregs of cold coffee. No. She knew what kind of cop he was, and she had lied to him, trying to protect her father, who had been a on the lump of lost possibilities, unbreachable differences. She had been determined that she wouldn't be like her mother. She had thought she didn't need to be protected, that she could act on her own and take the consequences. But she hadn't counted on those consequences being the endangerment of an innocent man. She hadn't counted on falling in love with a cop, on standing around outside a hospital room wondering what she would do if it were Marc lying in a hospital bed the way Sylvia Wilson's husband was.

"It can't ever work for us," she said. Her voice broke on the last word, as she met the concerned blue eyes whose gaze was almost as level as Marc's.

"He's a fine man," Sylvia said. "And the best partner Charlie ever had."

"I ... know that," Brooke said.

A good man. A good cop. And it was useless to hope he would ever understand her motives or forgive her actions. She wasn't sure she could forgive herself.

Brooke paid the cabbie, got out in front of her parents' house and slammed the cab door. She stood for a moment on the sidewalk, staring at the familiar front steps as the cab drove away. The cars that had lined the driveway earlier were gone, along with her brother's old model, and the quiet house had the relieved, after-the-party atmosphere it had always held after her parents' genial suburban gatherings. A wave of nostalgia, rife with memories of the safe and protected child she had been, caught her up for a moment.

When she looked back toward the front door, her mother's face was framed in the glass where she'd pulled back the lace curtains. She opened the door as Brooke started slowly up the walk.

"Brooke, dear, I wasn't expecting to see you. I was waiting for your call."

"Yes, I know, Mom. I got your message." She pressed her cheek to her mother's and put an arm around her shoulders, hugging her hard.

Her mother returned the hug, then stood back. Her gray eyes, so much like Brooke's, darkened with a hint of concern. "Are you all right, Brooke?"

"Yes, Mom. I'm fine. I just thought I'd talk to you in person rather than on the phone."

"Oh?"

Brooke managed a strained smile. "I had to come back for my car, anyway."

Watching her, her mother nodded slowly, then pulled the door shut behind them and turned to study her daughter, forehead creased in a little frown. "I thought you were with Marc, dear. I could have picked you up if I'd known you needed a ride."

Brooke turned away, busying herself with putting down her handbag and straightening the runner on the piano in the front hall. Finally she faced her mother. "Marc's partner was hurt tonight, Mom. In a fire. Marc's at Hartford General, visiting him."

"His partner?" Millie's fingertips flew to her throat. "Was he hurt badly?"

"No. He'll be all right."

"You saw him, then."

Brooke's glance met her mother's, then skittered off to the telephone table. "No, I . . . left while Marc was visiting him. I thought it would be easier if Marc didn't have to drive me here, so I . . . caught a cab." She went past the telephone into the brightly lit kitchen, as if its familiar comfort would give her the words she needed to ease her mother's worries—and her own.

The envelope, thick with money, was on the kitchen table in front of the butter dish. Brooke picked it up, then tightened her fingers around it convulsively as tears filled her eyes and blurred the familiar, well-loved room around her.

"Oh, Mom," she blurted out. "I miss Pop. Every time I come here, he's everywhere in the house. As if he were just gone for a few hours, and about to come home any time."

"Brooke, dear..." Her mother closed the distance between them and gathered Brooke into her arms.

Brooke wrapped her arms around her mother's shoulders, the envelope still clutched in one hand. "Mom," she said tearfully, "It must be so hard for you."

Surprised and troubled, Millie smoothed the back of Brooke's hair and made comforting, shushing sounds. "It's not so bad for me these days. I'm getting used to it. But Brooke, dear, what's upset you so much?"

Brooke drew in a shaky breath and didn't answer.

"Is it...the envelope?" Millie asked, with a hesitation in her voice.

Brooke wiped her eyes with the back of one hand, then drew back at arm's length. "Yes, Mom," she said. "It is. I knew about the envelope. I found it two weeks ago, when I was going through some of Pop's tax forms."

"But I don't understand. Why didn't you say something about it, Brooke? It's such a strange thing to find in his file cabinet."

Her mother's anxious face tugged at her emotions. Millie Shelburne had been through so much—and now this, on top of her grief and the daunting job of putting her life together. "I didn't want to worry you about it, Mom. Maybe it's just...Pop's nest egg, or emergency money, or...something. Lots of people keep money in file cabinets, Mom. Maybe he helped someone out with a loan, and he was just paid back...."

Millie's troubled, worried eyes searched her daughter's face. "But you don't think so, do you?"

"No, Mom." She dropped her eyes. "I don't." When she looked up again, her mother's face was stricken, as pale as the smudged envelope they'd both found.

Millie pressed a trembling hand to the collar of her blouse and spoke in a thin, strained voice. "You think your father was taking money...illegally?"

"Oh, Mom, I don't know what to think. Maybe it's not that. There could be a million reasons for Pop to have had that money. Maybe it's something completely innocent."

Her mother closed her eyes, tipped her head down for a moment, then nodded. "Perhaps you should tell your friend, Sergeant Lasaralle, Brooke."

"He...already knows, Mom."

Millie assessed her daughter pensively. "You told him when you found it?"

She shook her head, biting her lip. "I...meant to, but I didn't." She gave a small shrug, eloquent of deeds that should have been done, words that should have been said. "Anyway, he found out."

"And you . . . quarreled about it," her mother said.

Somehow the prim, old-fashioned phrase seemed to hold more hurt than any elaborate or enlightened explanations. Brooke nodded.

"It was my phone call, wasn't it?" her mother asked. At Brooke's hesitant silence, her mother made a sound of dismay in the back of her throat. "Oh, honey, I'm so sorry. I never should have said such a thing on the phone and to your answering machine."

"No, Mom, you *should* have. You did the right thing. You did what I should have done in the first place. I'm the one who concealed something I should have told Marc. I'm to blame for that." She drew in a deep breath, then let it out decisively. "I'm going to give him the envelope, Mom. I'll bring it to his house first thing in the morning. He wanted to see it."

"Then I suppose you should do that."

"Yes," Brooke said bleakly. There was a sharp stab of pain at the thought of facing Marc's censure again, but she pushed it aside and dredged up a brief smile for her mother. Glancing around at the remains of the softball get-together, she told her mother, "I'll finish cleaning up. Go put your feet up, Mom."

The eleven o'clock news had progressed from headlines to reports by the time Brooke finished straightening the kitchen and her mother called to her from the living room.

With the damp dish towel flung over her shoulder, she went into the front hall. Her mother was standing in the archway to the living room. The television was on.

"Brooke, is this the fire where Charlie was hurt?"

"Yes," Brooke replied, staring at the images on the screen. Unconsciously she reached for the support of the archway. The footage must have been taken after she'd left. The building was almost demolished, smoke and ashes pouring out of the dying fire. The turmoil of emotion she'd felt when she'd been there coursed through her again: fear for Charlie, deep dismay, the horrible familiarity of watching a building she'd worked in every day for a year burn to the ground.

Albert Andrews, suave and concerned as he spoke to the interviewer, stated that he was outraged at the possibility of arson and restated his support for law enforcement. It was a position he'd spelled out in a hundred press releases while she worked for him. She touched her fingers to her mouth, fighting back a sense of involvement that was too close, too threatening to acknowledge.

"Brooke, dear..." Her mother got up, crossed to the television and shut it off, then turned to face Brooke, her hands twisted together in front of her. "I think this might have something to do with your father."

"What, Mom?"

"I think, just before he died, he had something on his mind about Senator Andrews." She took a breath. "It was one night when he'd been on TV for something, and your father got up and slammed his hand against the side of the TV and shut it off. I thought he was going to knock it off the table. He said Andrews was no good. I told him he shouldn't say such a thing about his daughter's boss, and he said he had proof of it. That his daughter wasn't going to work for—" her mother shrugged one shoulder "—that creep, very much longer. He said, 'I'll do whatever I have to to get her out of there.'" Millie's glance, still worried but with a hint of decisiveness in the set of her brows, settled on Brooke. "I think he got you fired."

There was a hush of Sunday morning quiet over Marc's suburban neighborhood when Brooke made the turn onto his street, but her heart was thudding in a tempo that didn't fit the setting.

His car was parked in the driveway. So he was home. Brooke pulled up behind it and sat in the car for a moment, staring at his house, working up her courage to walk into it.

Coward, she berated herself, wiping her sweaty palms on the skirt of her dress. She reached for her pocketbook, where she'd stuffed the envelope, then hesitated again, closing her eyes and resting her forehead on the steering wheel.

Okay, Shelburne, you got yourself into this. No one else is going to get you out of it. So what are you waiting for?

She clutched her pocketbook tighter, then before she had a chance to change her mind, jerked the door handle, got out of the car and strode up the walk to Marc's front door.

She pressed the doorbell and quelled her panic by digging her fingernails into the palm of her hand. But she dreaded seeing the expression of anger and accusation she knew would be in his eyes when he looked at her.

So don't look at him!

When the door opened in front of her, she was staring at the threshold and at a pair of old running shoes and the cuffs of much-washed chinos. But her eyes traveled inevitably up past the wrinkles at his knees, the tails of a chambray shirt closed with two buttons across the chest, the V of a white T-shirt, to his face, with its dark, level gaze, unreadable as slate. If he'd had any reaction to seeing her there, it was gone by the time she could have seen it.

She forced her fingers to unclench from the strap of her pocketbook, fumbled with the flap and pulled out the worn white envelope. "I've brought this over," she said keeping her gaze fixed on the envelope.

He didn't move or speak. Dear God, would he never say anything? When she finally looked up at him, he was studying her, unblinking, his face still. There were lines of exhaustion around his mouth, tired creases around his eyes. He stepped back from the door, still silent, and held it open for her.

In the bright light from the living-room window, his exhaustion was unmistakable. For a span of heartbeats, her own tension dissolved in a rush of remorse and sympathy for Marc. Had he been up all night with Charlie? Her defenses momentarily forgotten, she stepped into the room and let him close the door behind her.

His gaze moved, finally, from her face to the envelope she clutched in her hand. "Thanks," he said, taking it. His voice sounded harsh, as if weariness or strain had roughened it.

She watched him study the envelope, still not opening it and riffling through the contents—the natural action of anyone presented with an envelope full of money.

"Is . . . Charlie all right?" she heard herself asking.

"Yes, he's fine." One corner of his mouth turned up in the suggestion of a smile, but it disappeared before it reached his eyes. "Complaining because he'll be out of commission and off the case for a few days." He passed a hand over his eyes, rubbing his temples. "When I came out from seeing Charlie, Sylvia told me you'd taken a cab home." His dark gaze, steady and piercing, fixed on her face again with a steadiness she read as accusation. "You could have told me yourself, Brooke."

"I thought you'd have things you had to do."

"You thought right."

The raw, determined anger in his voice hurt as much as his accusing gaze. *Oh, Marc. Forgive me. Touch me.* "Were you up all night?"

"Yes. I have a feeling about this case. That time is running out. That someone is about to get hurt." He drew in a sharp breath. "And I had some catching up to do."

Guilty, she folded her arms in front of her and turned her head away.

"I spent the night waking some people up, and I found some connections. Jack Lum, the man who owned Lum's News, is married to a cousin of Albert Andrews. He was running a small-time bookie operation out of the store and paying some people off. Maybe he was paying off your father, Brooke."

She stared down at her crossed arms for a moment, then gulped and looked up at him. "I have something else to tell you about this, something my mother said last night. Just before he died, my father told her he knew Andrews was no good. He had proof of it, he said. My mother thinks he got me fired. He didn't want me working for Andrews."

Marc's head came up, and his eyes narrowed. "He said he had proof? What proof?"

"I don't know."

There was a charged silence. She couldn't look at him.

"You don't know?" he said finally, almost softly, "or you're not saying?"

The false accusation stung even though she knew she deserved it. "If I knew anything, I'd tell you! Do you think I want anyone else to be hurt?"

"No, Brooke. I don't think you want anyone hurt. I don't think you wanted Charlie hurt. But if you'd told me everything you knew in the first place, maybe it wouldn't have happened."

"You think I don't know that?" She flung out a hand. "All right, I was wrong not to tell you. Is that what you want to hear?" His face blurred before her as angry tears formed in her eyes. "All right, I feel guilty as hell about it. About Charlie and about...about my father, too." She wiped her eyes with one hand. "I'm the one who was working for Andrews. I'm the one he got fired. You think I haven't wondered if I'm the reason he was shot? If maybe my father died because of me?"

"Brooke—"

"Well, I have!" She backed away from him, upset, confused, taking on guilt she didn't deserve because she blamed herself so bitterly for what she had done.

"Brooke, stop."

But she was beyond hearing him. She gave a convulsive sob, turned away from him and ran—from Marc, from her confusion, from herself.

"Brooke—"

She yanked the door open.

"Brooke, wait."

She ran down the stairs and across the driveway, ignoring the footsteps that followed her, intent only on getting to her car and escaping.

On the hood of her car was a package, wrapped in brown delivery paper and tied with a garish red ribbon. Without thought she reached to move it.

"Don't touch that!"

An iron-hard grip closed around her upper arm, and she was yanked back into the driveway so hard that her feet went out from under her, and her pocketbook slid off her shoulder and flew toward the car.

A split second later there was a crimson flash, a dull crack of explosives, and the hot, shocking fireworks of cardboard, brown paper, and incandescent flame that cracked the windshield of her car and rattled the steel of the hood.

Marc's cat shot out from between the front wheels with a yowl that drew out the cry frozen in her throat. Marc pulled her against him, burying her face in his shoulder, his arms tight around her, his cheek pressed against her hair.

She was trembling with shock, pulling in shuddering breaths that were not quite sobs. With one swift motion, Marc picked her up and carried her back into the house.

"Wh-what was it?" she stammered, her face against his chest.

She felt the tension in his arms and chest as he took a harsh breath to speak. "That was a calling card from some bastard who wanted to let me know he was around. If you had touched that thing, Brooke—" His arms tightened around her, and he swore softly. "If you had just touched it, it would have blown up in your face." His voice, already rough with adrenaline, hardened in controlled fury. "And it would have been my fault."

He kicked the door shut behind him without putting her down, then backed against it and let her slide down his body until she was standing in his arms, clinging to his shoulders as he cradled her against him and stroked the back of her hair. "God, Brooke, that was too close. That was just too close."

Brooke drew in a long, shaky breath, and then another, breathing in the warmth of Marc's body, the gentle caress of his hand, as if they were water and she were a grove of parched earth. "H-how did you know?"

His fingers splayed across her back. He swallowed convulsively. "I just knew."

She accepted the answer with no thought of questioning it. "And you knew something was going to happen."

"Yeah," he said, the word forced through gritted teeth. "I think I did. But it won't happen again, Brooke. I swear that. I won't let it happen again."

"It was f-from the people who k-killed my father, wasn't it?" she got out.

"Brooke, listen to me," he said urgently. He clasped her face in his palms and tipped her face up to meet his serious, intense gaze. "I'm going to take you out of this, make sure you're not connected to what's going on here. I know a lot of cops. I'm going to pull some strings to make sure nobody asks any questions about you or your family.''

''You're going to...'' The meaning of what he said seeped into her slowly, shocking her.

He pulled her head against his shoulder again. The hand at her back slowly stroked her spine. ''If they wanted to get to me, they did it. I won't risk you, Brooke. Not you. Nothing's worth that.''

''Oh, Marc,'' her heart was in her throat, and she felt the ache of tears behind her eyes. ''That's what they want, isn't it?''

His hands clasped her head again, tipping it back, and this time his mouth came down to hers with a hungry, ardent passion that stole her breath and stopped her heart for a moment. Her lips opened to his seeking tongue. She pressed against him, turning her body to meet his fully, straining to move closer, tightening her arms around him. He was hard, hot, aroused, and her own body responded to his need with urgency of her own.

The fantasy came almost immediately. She could smell the scent of tansy, hear the night wind in the enormous trees overhead. It blew through her hair as through the leaves, investing her with power and femininity, with force and strength of will to equal that of the man she loved, the man she had chosen.

She let power come to her with the heightening of her senses. She tuned herself to it, listened to it as if it could speak to her in words—the power she didn't have over the events of her life, the power this man was about to forego to keep her safe....

The wind blew through her like the force of life, sensuous, tangible. She cupped his face in her hands and slowly, agonizingly, drew away from him. She opened her eyes and met his gaze, dark with desire, burning through her, equal to her own fire.

"No." Her voice was ragged, but her gaze was as steady as his. She didn't let herself look away. "You can't let them do this, Marc. That's what they want. You can't give them what they want." Her eyes squeezed shut and a long, desperate breath came rushing out of her lungs. "*I* can't give them what they want. It won't work for us if we do that."

His fingers closed convulsively on her shoulders, then he lifted one hand to her face, stroking her cheek with his thumb.

He wanted her to look at him. She opened her eyes. He was gazing at her, troubled, questioning, intense.

"There's been enough covering up," she said, her voice determined, despite the tremor she couldn't quite control.

His thumb moved across her cheekbone, then still silent, he nodded once.

He didn't have to say more. Neither of them did.

Eleven

Her mother was on her knees in the flower border at the side of the house, a trowel in her hand, her face shiny with perspiration and scuffed with dirt.

"Mom?" At the quiet, tentative inquiry, Millie Shelburne sat back on her heels and turned her attention to her daughter.

"Mom, I—" She swallowed, not sure how to begin. "What . . . are you doing out here?"

Her mother's shoulders hunched, then fell again. She glanced at the half-dug border. "I decided to take out these day lilies. They've always been scraggly, anyway. Not enough sun."

"Oh." It was a small sound. "We looked all through the house for you. I couldn't imagine where you were."

Her mother glanced up at her, then straightened her shoulders determinedly. "I just felt like getting this done." She dug the trowel into the earth with inexpert force. "It's time I did get a few things done around here." Her gaze moved up to Brooke's face again. "You gave Sergeant Lasaralle the envelope?"

Brooke nodded. "He's here with me. In Pop's office."

"That's...that's good," Millie said, but her chin was set as if she were determined not to let it tremble, and she grasped the stem of the overgrown plant with angry force. "I just want to get this...one—" she tugged at it "—plant...out." She took a breath. "These things are like...pulling...teeth. I couldn't find the shovel. I don't know where your father kept all the garden tools."

Brooke settled to her knees on the lawn, newly mowed by Billy for the cookout, watching her mother wrestle with the overgrown, deep-rooted plant. "Mom, I need to talk to you, about—"

Her mother stopped digging and glanced at her, one hand still wrapped around the tough, woody base of the plant.

"About Pop, and what he was involved in. Whatever it was, Mom, I think it's still going on. I think it had something to do with Andrews and the fire last night." She stopped again, then closed her eyes, unable to look at her mother's face, knowing the worried look she was going to see there. *Dear God, this was hard.* "Mom, somebody tried to warn Marc off the case. They tried to set a bomb at his house."

Millie made a startled, horrified sound.

Brooke made herself open her eyes. "The fire at the headquarters was started with a bomb, Mom. And the one at Lum's. Marc thinks the same people are behind them."

"But who?" Millie's gaze was fixed on Brooke while she slowly brushed a hand across her face, wiping one smudge of dirt, leaving another.

"We don't know, Mom. Not yet."

Her mother's glance shifted toward the backyard. Brooke turned to see Marc coming around the corner of the house, hands in his pockets, long legs covering the distance toward them with slow, easy strides. Millie watched him as he crouched down beside Brooke, unhurried, with the patience to wait until she was ready to speak.

Millie's lip trembled, and she caught it between her teeth before turning back to the flower border. She shoved the trowel viciously into the soil around the stubborn roots, yanked at the resisting day lily, then sat back again and let her hands fall still. "I think I knew he was doing something he hated," she said.

"He told you that?" Marc asked her.

Millie shook her head, her eyes fixed on the garden. "No. But I knew anyway. When you love someone, you always know, I guess, one way or another."

Brooke felt a lump rise in her throat, stopping her from speaking.

"Just before he died, I thought he had resolved it in his mind." Millie turned her gaze toward Marc. "That night he told me he was going to get Brooke out of the senator's office, he said he had plenty of proof. Those were his words. 'Plenty of proof.'"

"Mrs. Shelburne," Marc said levelly, "we can't pin anything on Andrews. But I think if we had some leverage, we might be able to make someone in this case crack. Would you be willing to testify to that in court if you had to? What your husband said?"

"To testify?"

Marc's level gaze held hers. "I can't promise that you wouldn't be putting yourself in danger," he told her. "But I can order police protection for you until this is over."

"Marc—" Brooke started in protest.

He glanced at her but spoke again to Millie. "Will you do it?"

Millie let out a breath. Her eyes turned back to the unfinished job in front of her. "If you think it will do any good, then I guess I'd be willing." Her hands tugged at the stubborn plant again. "Damn this thing," she muttered, a hint of tears in her voice. She yanked at it, pulling with all her strength, then rose to one knee and yanked again. The roots strained, then snapped, spraying soil over the foundation, the lawn and the three people there.

The older woman rocked back onto her seat with a grunt of surprise, then gave a long huff of breath as Marc reached to help her up. She dropped the plant onto the loose dirt, then dusted her hands. The gesture slowed, then stopped as she glanced at Brooke and then Marc. "Thank you," she said finally, with dignity.

Brooke was sitting in the sultry darkness on her terrace, the portable phone beside her, when she heard his car turn onto her street. It stopped opposite her apartment, and a door slammed. Her senses were over-acute, honed by anxiety and waiting, and she recognized the pattern of Marc's footsteps, then the rumble of his voice. He must have stopped to speak to the uniformed police officer he'd stationed outside her apartment.

She sat where she was for a moment, unmoving in the darkness, then got up to let him in.

She was standing in the open doorway, holding the edge of the door with both hands, when he climbed the outside stairs, then paused at the landing, leaning one shoulder against the doorway, his eyes fixed on Brooke.

It was too hot in her apartment for lights; the kitchen was illuminated only by the subdued glow of a night lamp. They stood utterly still, both of them caught in a moment of suspended time. The dim, golden light played over his face, the sharp line of his jaw, the random creases in his oxford shirt. The pattern of his knuckles inside the pockets of faded chinos was strongly visible.

As if the spell were broken when she noticed his clenched fists, he spoke. "It's over," he said, his voice husky. "I could have called you, but I didn't want to take the time to do it. I wanted to see you."

The rough timbre of his voice touched some point in the center of her chest and sent slow, gentle shivers radiating out to the surface of her skin. "I . . . needed to see you, too," she admitted huskily. Her hands tightened their hold on the door, as if to keep herself from touching him as he walked by her into the kitchen.

In the closer lamplight, the lines of fatigue around his eyes were more visible, but he gave off tense, controlled energy that belied the weariness he must be feeling.

She shut the door and pushed her hands into the pockets of her skirt in a posture that matched his. "Tell me about it."

"Jack Lum cracked when we convinced him your father had left testimony that could probably link him to murder. He spilled the whole story. Enough, I think, to get Andrews convicted. It worked."

"Oh, Marc." She let out a long breath.

"Lum's been making 'contributions' to Andrews for years," Marc went on, "in exchange for Andrews turning a blind eye on the operation." His voice hardened. "Apparently Andrews's 'clean government' was funded by a lot of dirty money. I think he had quite a few questionable contributors, but it will be almost impossible to trace them now. All the records were in the headquarters building that burned last night."

Brooke glanced down at her feet, then looked up at Marc again. "Andrews," she said musingly. "I guess I'm not a very good judge of character. I worked for him for months." She dropped her gaze again. Silence stretched out between them, heavy with long-resisted truths. "What about my father?" she said finally.

"Brooke . . . come closer. I need to touch you."

The words were said with no more quiet emphasis than he'd used in telling her about Andrews, but every cell of her body went into a crazy dance of response that cared about nothing—not the turbulent events of the day, not the questions—nothing save the overriding need to be closer to him. She took the two steps that put her in front of him. Slowly, he drew his hands out of his pockets and raised them to her shoulders. He tipped his head toward hers, touching only foreheads, but her whole being responded with a flush of heat and a wash of awareness.

"Let's go somewhere we can sit, in the dark," he murmured.

"Yes." She turned and put her hand on his waist. He draped his arm around her shoulders as they walked toward her bedroom. At the doorway she went ahead. His palm found the center of her spine and caressed it. They brushed past the potted herbs on the bench and went outside, trailed by the scent of the plants.

The blanket she'd been sitting on was a pale blur on the slates. Marc urged her down beside him with a hand around her hips. His arm circled her shoulders as she sat beside him, leaning back against the painted clapboards of the wall.

Marc's hand moved against her head, his fingertips starting a slow, sensual stroking through her hair.

"Your father figured out what was going on at Jack Lum's and with Andrews," he said. His voice was a gruff rumble near her ear. "He didn't want to play ball with them at first, but Andrews threatened to drag you through the mud with him if anybody blew the whistle on him. He went along with them to protect you, Brooke."

She made a sound that was barely more than a breath, but Marc's fingers stilled in her hair.

"Hold my hand, Brooke," he told her.

She lifted her hand to her shoulder, and his grasp closed around it, making warm, firm contact. "He took the money, I think, because they wouldn't have trusted him to keep quiet otherwise. But I think he'd decided to give it back at the end. He wasn't supposed to be at Lum's the night he was shot. I think he might have gone there to tell them the deal was off."

A breeze stirred the leaves of the elm in the yard and the potted herbs on the terrace. Against the screen of her window, a June bug knocked and buzzed, attracted by the faint light from the kitchen.

"Who shot my father?" Brooke asked.

"Andrews had some of the local hoods in his pocket. One of them was paying a night visit to Lum's to plant a little warning that his payment was due. Your father caught him."

There was another silence, filled with night sounds and the strong, steady warmth of Marc's hand on hers. She gathered her feet beneath her. "I'd better call my mother."

"Billy's with her."

She glanced toward him, meeting his eyes for the first time since they'd come out, her own gaze wide and surprised.

"I told him as soon as I filed the report. I didn't want him to hear it from anyone else on the force. He's at your mother's house now."

"Thank you for thinking of that. Of Billy."

"You all right?" he asked.

"I'm glad it's over." She let her head tip back on his arm, then turned her face slightly toward him, to study the clean three-quarter profile, wondering if that was an answer. *All right* didn't really describe what she was. She was . . . aware—of the soft, heavy night air, the fragrance of aromatic plants, the texture of Marc's muscles, the way his breath sighed out through his teeth and his eyes slid shut for a moment, emphasizing the fatigue lines.

Her heart went out to him, realizing how weary he must be. "You've been up thirty-six hours, Marc. You must need sleep."

His fingers traced the edge of her earlobe, followed the line of her jaw in a whisper-light caress that brought her face closer to his. A slow, intimate smile tipped up the corners of his mouth. "Sleep isn't what I need."

Feeling his breath on her face, watching his eyes, she grew giddily aware of her own needs, of the cadence of her own breathing, her quickened pulse, the drift of reaction that spread through her, sensitizing the whole surface of her skin.

His lips brushed hers with gentle pressure. Her lips parted, her mouth seeking, nuzzling, exploring with slow, light sensuality, until the need for more became a sound in her throat, then a shared sound as he turned and lowered her to the blanket. His mouth didn't leave hers as he half covered her body with his. "You're what I need, Brooke," he murmured against her mouth. "This is what I need."

Her arm slid around his neck as she opened her mouth to the sleek, hot invasion of his tongue. He plundered the sensitive, intimate surfaces of her mouth, and she welcomed the plundering, her tongue meeting his in a wholly sensual mating that spread heat throughout her body. She arched against him, seeking closer contact, straining against him while their mouths met and matched and claimed.

She felt his fingers unfastening the buttons of her dress, grazing her skin. She stroked his back, then tugged impatiently at his shirt. It came out, and she smoothed her palms inside, seeking the warm, resilient texture of his skin, reveling in his response to her touch.

He loosened the last fastening at her shoulder and lifted himself above her to remove her dress.

"Here?" she said, smiling.

One corner of his mouth turned up. "Yes. Here. Now."

"I *live* in this neighborhood."

"I know. But you live behind so many damn plants, no one could see us if it were broad daylight."

His wrist brushed her nipple through the lace of her bra. The peak of her breast hardened into a tight, eager knot of desire. Her hands clenched on his back.

He leaned over her, and she felt his warm, moist breath at the center of her collarbones. "Tell me about your plants," he said against her skin. "What are they?"

"The names?"

"Mmm."

The frothy leaves of one of her herbs arched above them, framing the portion of summer sky she could see beyond the roof line. "Yarrow," she murmured. Her gaze drifted to the tiny leaved stalks of the mint plants. "Pennyroyal. Peppermint."

His mouth, barely touching her skin, moved lower, warming her skin. "What else?"

She smiled. "Woad. Sweet cicely."

His deft hands slid under her back, lifting her to unclasp her bra. The scrap of material was eased down her arms and dropped on the blanket beside them while he settled her back on the blanket.

Her breasts felt heavy, full of yearning as the night air touched them, the nipples, hard and erect, waited for the warmth of Marc's hands. But he touched her with eyes only, sliding his thumb, then the back of his knuckles along the outer edge of her breasts, drawing a soft sound from her throat.

Her hands, eager and seeking, undid the buttons of his shirt, then spread over his bare chest, pushing the shirt back from his shoulders, impatient with the barriers.

He sat back on his heels to shrug off the shirt, then suddenly took her hand and tugged her up to her knees beside him. Her loose dress went slithering down past her hips. Marc let go of her hand, studying her. She could just make out his features. The backs of his knuckles traced her jaw, her shoulders, then his warm palms brushed the sides of her rib cage, tracing the curve of her waist and hips while her eyelids drifted closed and shivers of yearning started in her breasts and thighs.

They were kneeling in front of the open door. Marc leaned into the room and plucked a fernlike leaf from a plant on the bench. "And what's this one?" he murmured. He brought his hand in front of his chest, closing his fist to crush the leaf, then opening it slowly. Fragrance enveloped her.

"Tansy."

He touched it to her neck, her shoulder, the valley between her breasts.

Brooke reached for the snap of his pants, her fingers deft, the gesture graceful with feminine power, sure of her needs, sure of the needs of her lover.

He stood to strip off his chinos, then knelt before her again and lowered her beneath him. Soft, warm earth, blanketed with the lush growth of midsummer, caressed, welcomed, whispered of pleasure. His hand slipped under the wisp of lace across the lower part of her stomach, and she raised her hips to let him slip it off.

The wind, restless in the leaves overhead, whispered over their naked skin, cooling and inflaming at once. Touched by it, Brooke shivered. There was a sweet, aching need in her breasts that could be met only by the warm, silken depths of his mouth. When he lowered his head to touch her, first with tongue and lips, then all of his mouth as he drew her nipple into its warm, wet depths, she arched toward him and moaned softly, deep in her throat.

She cradled his hips, then his wide shoulders and the distinct, ridged muscles of his upper chest. She urged him onto his back, and he complied, letting her bid him, letting his eyes close, though his chest lifted and fell in rapid, aroused breaths.

Heady with pleasure given and received, she touched and tempted, relearning his body, freeing her own sensuality with every caress and every response. When her hand closed around the warm, smooth shaft of his masculinity, he sucked in a harsh breath and held it for a long moment, then let it out in a rush as his fingers closed around her shoulder and he pulled her down beside him.

They spoke in the music of body and spirit, sleek wet mouths and seeking hands. He kissed the hollow beneath her chin, then trailed kisses along her collarbone, between her breasts, in the soft dip of her waist. Her hands threaded into the thick texture of his hair. Her head tipped back, and her lips parted as she felt her gathering desire like a warm flame licking through her.

When his hips sought the cradle of her thighs, she moved to accommodate him, guiding him with her hands, letting him know her needs, her wants. Her name was a hoarse litany of praise and adulation in his voice. He joined their bodies in the slow, ancient rhythm of sensuality that drew in and joined their spirits and erased the boundaries of time and space, of real and imagined, of body and mind. They moved, beat for beat, toward a consummation that was in equal measure ancient and present, given and taken, male and female, earthly and ethereal. And when the shattering completion came, Brooke felt his ecstasy and her own as one, magnified a thousandfold by her fierce and tender love, and by the fierce and tender love she knew he returned to her.

Long moments later, washed in satisfaction, they lay together while he swept his fingers through her hair in slow, sated strokes.

"Marc."

She felt his smile against her shoulder. "Mmm?"

"I think being in someone's mind—it's not what I expected."

His hand stilled. "What is it, then?"

"It's like a wonderful freedom. Like the place I was always meant to be."

He braced himself on an elbow to lean over her and kiss her. "I want you in my mind, Brooke. I want you in my life. Everywhere."

She didn't have to answer. She smiled. She touched his hand. He knew.

*   *   *   *   *

The tradition continues this month as Silhouette presents its fifth annual Christmas collection

SILHOUETTE Christmas STORIES 1990

The romance of Christmas sparkles in four enchanting stories written by some of your favorite Silhouette authors:

Ann Major * SANTA'S SPECIAL MIRACLE
Rita Rainville * LIGHTS OUT!
Lindsay McKenna * ALWAYS AND FOREVER
Kathleen Creighton * THE MYSTERIOUS GIFT

Spend the holidays with Silhouette and discover the special magic of falling in love in this heartwarming Christmas collection.

SILHOUETTE CHRISTMAS STORIES 1990 is available now at your favorite retail outlet, or order your copy by sending your name, address, zip or postal code along with a check or money order for $4.50, plus 75¢ postage and handling, payable to Silhouette Books to:

In the U.S.
3010 Walden Ave.,
P.O. Box 1396
Buffalo, NY 14269-1396

In Canada
P.O. Box 609
Fort Erie, ON
L2A 5X3

Please specify book title with your order.

SX90-1A

ARE YOU A ROMANCE READER WITH OPINIONS?

Openings are currently available for participation in the 1990-1991 Romance Reader Panel. We are looking for new participants from all regions of the country and from all age ranges.

If selected, you will be polled once a month by mail to comment on new books you have recently purchased, and may occasionally be asked for more in-depth comments. Individual responses will remain confidential and all postage will be prepaid.

Regular purchasers of one favorite series, as well as those who sample a variety of lines each month, are needed, so fill out and return this application today for more detailed information.

1. Please indicate the romance series you purchase from regularly at retail outlets.

Harlequin	Silhouette	
1. ☐ Romance	6. ☐ Romance	10. ☐ Bantam Loveswept
2. ☐ Presents	7. ☐ Special Edition	11. ☐ Other _____
3. ☐ American Romance	8. ☐ Intimate Moments	
4. ☐ Temptation	9. ☐ Desire	
5. ☐ Superromance		

2. Number of romance paperbacks you purchase new in an average month:

   12.1 ☐ 1 to 4   .2 ☐ 5 to 10   .3 ☐ 11 to 15   .4 ☐ 16+

3. Do you currently buy romance   13.1 ☐ yes   .2 ☐ no
   series through direct mail?

   If yes, please indicate series: _____
                                    (14,15)   (16,17)

4. Date of birth: _____ / _____ / _____
            (Month)   (Day)   (Year)
            18,19   20,21   22,23

5. Please print:
   Name: _____
   Address: _____
   City: _____ State: _____ Zip: _____
   Telephone No. (optional): (_____) _____

MAIL TO: Attention: Romance Reader Panel
            Consumer Opinion Center
            P.O. Box 1395
            Buffalo, NY 14240-9961

Office Use Only   DDK

Take 4 bestselling love stories FREE

Plus get a FREE surprise gift!

PASSPORT TO ROMANCE
SWEEPSTAKES RULES

1. **HOW TO ENTER:** To enter, you must be the age of majority and complete the official entry form, or print your name, address, telephone number and age on a plain piece of paper and mail to: Passport to Romance, P.O. Box 9056, Buffalo, NY 14269-9056. No mechanically reproduced entries accepted.

2. All entries must be received by the CONTEST CLOSING DATE, DECEMBER 31, 1990 TO BE ELIGIBLE.

3. **THE PRIZES:** There will be ten (10) Grand Prizes awarded, each consisting of a choice of a trip for two people from the following list:
   i) London, England (approximate retail value $5,050 U.S.)
   ii) England, Wales and Scotland (approximate retail value $6,400 U.S.)
   iii) Carribean Cruise (approximate retail value $7,300 U.S.)
   iv) Hawaii (approximate retail value $9,550 U.S.)
   v) Greek Island Cruise in the Mediterranean (approximate retail value $12,250 U.S.)
   vi) France (approximate retail value $7,300 U.S.)

4. Any winner may choose to receive any trip or a cash alternative prize of $5,000.00 U.S. in lieu of the trip.

5. **GENERAL RULES:** Odds of winning depend on number of entries received.

6. A random draw will be made by Nielsen Promotion Services, an independent judging organization, on January 29, 1991, in Buffalo, NY, at 11:30 a.m. from all eligible entries received on or before the Contest Closing Date.

7. Any Canadian entrants who are selected must correctly answer a time-limited, mathematical skill-testing question in order to win.

8. Full contest rules may be obtained by sending a stamped, self-addressed envelope to: "Passport to Romance Rules Request", P.O. Box 9998, Saint John, New Brunswick, Canada E2L 4N4.

9. Quebec residents may submit any litigation respecting the conduct and awarding of a prize in this contest to the Régie des loteries et courses du Québec.

10. Payment of taxes other than air and hotel taxes is the sole responsibility of the winner.

11. Void where prohibited by law.

COUPON BOOKLET OFFER TERMS

To receive your Free travel-savings coupon booklets, complete the mail-in Offer Certificate on the preceeding page, including the necessary number of proofs-of-purchase, and mail to: Passport to Romance, P.O. Box 9057, Buffalo, NY 14269-9057. The coupon booklets include savings on travel-related products such as car rentals, hotels, cruises, flowers and restaurants. Some restrictions apply. The offer is available in the United States and Canada. Requests must be postmarked by January 25, 1991. Only proofs-of-purchase from specially marked "Passport to Romance" Harlequin® or Silhouette® books will be accepted. The offer certificate must accompany your request and may not be reproduced in any manner. Offer void where prohibited or restricted by law. LIMIT FOUR COUPON BOOKLETS PER NAME, FAMILY, GROUP, ORGANIZATION OR ADDRESS. Please allow up to 8 weeks after receipt of order for shipment. Enter quickly as quantities are limited. Unfulfilled mail-in offer requests will receive free Harlequin® or Silhouette® books (not previously available in retail stores), in quantities equal to the number of proofs-of-purchase required for Levels One to Four, as applicable.

OFFICIAL SWEEPSTAKES
ENTRY FORM

Complete and return this Entry Form immediately—the more Entry Forms you submit, the better your chances of winning!
- Entry Forms must be received by **December 31, 1990**
- A random draw will take place on **January 29, 1991**
- Trip must be taken by **December 31, 1991**

3-SD-3-SW

YES, I want to win a PASSPORT TO ROMANCE vacation for two! I understand the prize includes round-trip air fare, accommodation and a daily spending allowance.

Name_____

Address_____

City_____ State_____ Zip_____

Telephone Number_____ Age_____

Return entries to: **PASSPORT TO ROMANCE**, P.O. Box 9056, Buffalo, NY 14269-9056

© 1990 Harlequin Enterprises Limited

COUPON BOOKLET/OFFER CERTIFICATE

Item	LEVEL ONE Booklet 1	LEVEL TWO Booklet 1 & 2	LEVEL THREE Booklet 1, 2 & 3	LEVEL FOUR Booklet 1, 2, 3 & 4
Booklet 1 = $100+	$100+	$100+	$100+	$100+
Booklet 2 = $200+		$200+	$200+	$200+
Booklet 3 = $300+			$300+	$300+
Booklet 4 = $400+	_____	_____	_____	$400+
Approximate Total Value of Savings	$100+	$300+	$600+	$1,000+
# of Proofs of Purchase Required	4	6	12	18
Check One	_____	_____	_____	_____

Name_____

Address_____

City_____ State_____ Zip_____

Return Offer Certificates to: **PASSPORT TO ROMANCE**, P.O. Box 9057, Buffalo, NY 14269-9057

Requests must be postmarked by **January 25, 1991**

✂

ONE PROOF OF PURCHASE

3-SD-3

To collect your free coupon booklet you must include the necessary number of proofs-of-purchase with a properly completed Offer Certificate

© 1990 Harlequin Enterprises Limited

See previous page for details